DEKOK AND THE
BEGGING DEATH

"DeKok" Books by A.C. Baantjer:

Published in the United States:
Murder in Amsterdam
DeKok and the Sunday Strangler
DeKok and the Corpse on Christmas Eve
DeKok and the Somber Nude
DeKok and the Dead Harlequin
DeKok and the Sorrowing Tomcat
DeKok and the Disillusioned Corpse
DeKok and the Careful Killer
DeKok and the Romantic Murder
DeKok and the Dying Stroller
DeKok and the Corpse at the Church Wall
DeKok and the Dancing Death
DeKok and the Naked Lady
DeKok and the Brothers of the Easy Death
DeKok and the Deadly Accord
DeKok and Murder in Seance
DeKok and Murder in Ecstasy
DeKok and the Begging Death
DeKok and Murder on the Menu

Available soon from InterContinental Publishing:
DeKok and the Geese of Death
DeKok and Murder by Melody
DeKok and Death of a Clown
DeKok and Variations on Murder
DeKok and Murder by Installments
DeKok and Murder on Blood Mountain
DeKok and the Dead Lovers
DeKok and the Mask of Death
DeKok and the Corpse by Return
DeKok and Murder in Bronze
DeKok and the Deadly Warning
DeKok and Murder First Class
DeKok and the Vendetta
DeKok and Murder Depicted
DeKok and Dance Macabre
DeKok and the Disfiguring Death
DeKok and the Devil's Conspiracy
DeKok and the Duel at Night
and more . . .

DeKok
and the
Begging Death

by
BAANTJER

translated from the Dutch by H.G. Smittenaar

INTERCONTINENTAL PUBLISHING

ISBN 1 881164 17 9

DEKOK AND THE BEGGING DEATH. English translation copyright
© 1999 by InterContinental Publishing Inc. Translated from *De Cock en*
de smekende dood, by Baantjer [Albert Cornelis Baantjer], copyright ©
1982 by Uitgeverij De Fontein, Baarn, Netherlands. All rights reserved.
Printed in the United States of America. No part of this book may be used
or reproduced in any manner whatsoever without written permission
except in the case of brief quotations embodied in critical articles or
reviews. For information address InterContinental Publishing, Box 7242,
Fairfax Station, Virginia, 22039.

Printing History:
       1st Dutch printing: 1982
       17th Dutch printing: 1998

       1st American edition:1999

Typography: Monica S. Rozier, Woodbridge, VA
Cover by: Rosemary Boyd of Document Design, Laguna Beach, CA
Manufactured by: BookCrafters, Fredericksburg, VA

Library of Congress Cataloging-in-Publication Data

Baantjer, A. C.
    [De Cock en de smekende dood.   English]
    DeKok and the Begging Death / by Baantjer ; translated from the
Dutch by H.G. Smittenaar. — 1st American ed.
       p.   cm.
    ISBN 1-881164-17-9
    I. Smittenaar, H. G.   II. Title
PT5881.12.A2C622813   1999
839.3'1364—dc21   98-45858
                                                              CIP

***DeKok
and the
Begging Death***

1

A tall, dignified minister spoke from the intricately carved pulpit in the old Wester Church in Amsterdam. A hesitant beam of sunlight penetrated through a high window and playfully illuminated the black robe, giving it a multi-colored luster. The minister adjusted his garment slightly and with careful, calculated movements placed his horn-rimmed glasses on his nose. He looked down at the congregation before him. There was something arrogant in the look. With a slight cough he leaned his head backward as if to increase the distance between himself and the congregation below him.

"The text for today," he said with a trained voice, "is from the book of Isaiah, chapter forty-three, verse one: *I have called thee by thy name; thou art Mine.*"

The words echoed against the soundboard of the pulpit and descended, laden with meaning, upon the heads of the congregation.

Detective-Inspector DeKok (Homicide) of the old station house in Warmoes Street was seated on a wooden bench. It had been some time since he had visited a church. He tried to think back. He was still a child when he accompanied his grandparents to church on the former island of Urk. He remembered the best part of those services was the peppermint he was allowed to eat during the service. As soon as he was seated between his grand-parents on the narrow benches in the village church, his grand-mother would hand him a peppermint. When he had silently dissolved it in his mouth, his grandfather would hand him another one. Those were happy days.

With a sigh he returned to the present and pulled the wool, scarf from around his neck and placed it next to him on the bench. He placed his old, decrepit, little hat on top of the scarf. Vledder, next to him, looked irritated.

"What *are* we doing here?" he hissed.

DeKok studied his young friend, assistant and fellow inspector with a benign smile.

"We are attending a church service," he answered, a surprised look on his face. "A child is being baptized."

Vledder snorted.

"And for that I have to sacrifice my Sunday off?"

"Yes," nodded DeKok complacently. "We have been invited."

An unbelieving look appeared on Vledder's face.

"We have been invited?" he asked. "To attend a baptism?"

His voice was louder than he intended. A few people looked around with annoyed faces.

DeKok pressed his index finger to his lips. Then he made a hidden gesture at the pulpit.

"Shh," he warned. "It is very ill-mannered to cause a disturbance when God's word is being declared."

"I'm a heathen," said Vledder, but softly.

DeKok did not react. He slid further down on the bench and pressed his knees against the back of the seats in front of him. The resounding tones of the pastor, made him sleepy. With an effort he squinted his eyes closed and shook his head. Then he opened his eyes again, banning all thoughts of slumber.

After a relatively short speech, the pastor descended from the pulpit and approached the baptismal fount. A group of children joined him there.

A gray-haired man in impeccable morning clothes appeared from a side door. He carried a baby in a long, silk creation on his right arm. The child produced complaining baby sounds. A notable tenderness seemed to descend on the congregation.

With an awkward gesture the old man handed the child to a young, blonde woman who had been waiting next to the cleric.

Vledder nudged DeKok.

"Who's that child?" he whispered.

The gray sleuth did not answer.

The parson dipped two fingers into the water of the fount and placed the dripping fingers on the forehead of the baby.

"Albert Cornelis," he said majestically, "I baptize thee in the name of the Father, and the Son, and the Holy Spirit."

"Who is that child?" repeated Vledder, more insistent than the first time.

DeKok whispered back.

"You heard ... Albert Cornelis ... grandson of the old gentleman in morning clothes."

"And who is that?"

DeKok smiled.

"In his profane self ... I mean when he is not holding up children for baptism, he's the Managing Director of the Ysselstein Bank on Emperors Canal. His name is Albert Cornelis Verbruggen. The baby has been named after him."

"And who invited us? He?"

DeKok shook his head.

"Not directly."

"Then ... who?"

Organ music filled the church. The congregation stood. De-

Kok joined in the singing of the Psalm.

Vledder looked with surprise at his old friend and mentor. The power of the melodious baritone surprised him. DeKok was known to hum Christmas Carols from time to time, regardless of the time of year, but this was the first time that Vledder had heard him sing.

When the singing stopped and the congregation was seated again, DeKok leaned over to Vledder.

"Mr. Verbruggen has received threatening letters," he whispered.

"From whom?"

DeKok shrugged his shoulders.

"I know too little at this time. Commissaris Buitendam called me at home this morning. He had been contacted by Mr. Schaap."

"The Judge-Advocate?"

DeKok nodded.

"Mr. Verbruggen had contacted *him* in turn with an urgent request for protection. It has been threatened that the child is to be kidnapped."

Vledder frowned.

"The little baby we just saw?"

"Yes."

"Here!?"

DeKok pushed out his lower lip and nodded.

"During the service," he said. "I barely had time to organize anything at all. I had to fight with the Watch Commander* to get ten constables. Eight of them are surrounding the church and two

---

* Watch-Commander, i.e *desk-sergeant*, occupies roughly the same function as a desk-sergeant in the United States, but is also responsible for disposition of extra personnel, including officers superior in rank. For some unfathomable reason also referred to as *Brigadier* or *Brigges*, for short.

of them are with the sexton, his wife and, of course, the baby in the vestry."

Vledder shook his head.

"Kidnapping," he said hoarsely. "In a church and during the baptism?" There was disbelief and confusion in his voice.

Again the organ sounded and the congregation started on the final Psalm.

This time DeKok did not sing along. His gaze travelled across the backs in front of him. The first pews, he thought, seemed pretty well occupied by the family, relatives and friends of the bank director.

To the left, also immaculate in a morning costume, was Mr. Schaap, the Judge-Advocate. DeKok raised an eyebrow in silent surprise to find him there. Strange that he should be here, he mused. Highly unusual. Although, by Law, the Judge-Advocate is considered to be the investigating officer of preference, in practice Mr. Schaap had a habit of staying in the background. He seldom, if ever, appeared in public, not even for the most intriguing murder cases.

DeKok grinned to himself. He did not really care whether the Judge-Advocate was present, or not. In his long career he had developed a routine of going his own way. Secure in his seniority and with total absence of ambition for promotion, he solved his cases ... usually in direct opposition to the instructions of his nominal superiors in rank.

His gaze drifted to other people. He was looking for something that did not fit, something that would jar in the formal surroundings. He listened for a dissonance in the singing, but the congregation sounded exactly as it should, a devout gathering of interested persons celebrating the baptism of a new soul.

Finally, with arms spread wide, the parson spoke the blessing which elicited a resounding "Amen" from the gathering. Mr.

Verbruggen, his daughter and son-in-law stood below the pulpit, ready to lead the procession to the vestibule of the church.

From a distance DeKok looked at the faces which were now all turned more or less in his direction. The entire assembly would have to pass him on the way out. Apart from the Judge-Advocate, he did not recognize a single face.

On an impulse, he motioned toward Vledder to remain where he was, while he hastened to the vestry. Both constables were alert and the sexton's wife looked with a warm smile at the baby who was fast asleep. For the moment DeKok was satisfied.

He made his way back to Vledder. After the last congratulations in the vestibule has been exchanged, both cops approached the reception line.

DeKok inclined his head to the mother, while he studied her face intently. A beautiful woman, he thought. The face was delicate and yet strongly molded, but there was a look of infinite sadness in the eyes. The hazel eyes did not shine and the purplish-dark rings under the eyes were barely concealed by a cunning and expensive make-up.

"My name is DeKok," he announced himself. "DeKok ... with kay-oh-kay." He indicated Vledder. "This is my partner, Vledder. We are police Inspectors."

She looked at him with a question in her sad eyes.

"Police?"

DeKok nodded slowly. He noticed with sudden concern how the young woman paled under her make-up. She faltered. Her eyes turned up and then she collapsed sideways against the young man next to her.

Quickly DeKok kneeled down next to her. With the back of his hand he touched her cheeks. While he supported her head, he looked at Vledder.

"An ambulance, quick," he barked.

* * *

"How's she doing?"

Vledder made a helpless gesture.

"It's too soon to tell. She's in shock and she's in intensive care. Apparently, according to the doctor, she's also physically in a very weak condition."

"How's that?"

Vledder shrugged.

"It has something to do with her state of mind. After I left the hospital, I stopped by the church. I'd promised the sexton's wife that I would let her know. She was upset too. She told me that the baptism had been postponed once already because of an illness of Mrs. LaCroix."

"LaCroix?"

Vledder nodded.

"That's her name now. Her husband is Henri LaCroix. They've been married for about eighteen months."

"Happily?"

"According to my sources there was no indication of anything but a happy marriage. The couple seemed very content. They went to church regularly, every Sunday. Only after the child was born did that change. Henri was often alone. When the sexton's wife asked about it, Henri told her that his wife was afraid to leave the house. She was pathologically afraid that something would happen to her baby. Often she did not sleep at night, but kept a watch over the child."

"Where do they live?"

"Churchill Lane."

DeKok pulled out his lower lip and let it plop back. He repeated the annoying gesture several times.

"Very strange. As soon as Mrs. LaCroix is able to talk to us,

13

we'll have to ask her about it. There has to be a reason for this sudden fear."

Vledder pulled up a chair.

"The threatening letters, maybe?"

DeKok shook his head.

"No, those letters are a recent phenomenon. And the baby is already five months old." He opened a drawer in his desk and took out two envelopes. "Mr. Verbruggen gave these to me," he explained. "But then," he added, "the letters are addressed to him."

Vledder waited patiently.

"It was chaos in the church," continued DeKok after a while. "I only had time for a few words with Verbruggen. He was very upset and to tell you the truth, I was glad to see him disappear as quickly as possible. He, his son-in-law and the baby went to Laren. That's where he lives," he added.

Vledder watched as DeKok unearthed a piece of licorice from the still open drawer. The older man put it in his mouth and chewed thoughtfully for a while.

"I made sure that the car had a police escort. That's all I could do at the time. Of course, I also notified the Laren police. They promised to keep an eye on things."

Vledder was studying the envelopes.

"They have been mailed by regular mail," he observed. "Mailed in Amsterdam," he added. Then he looked up. "Of course, you had it checked for prints?"

DeKok nodded thoughtfully.

"It was the first thing I did. There were several usable prints. They still have to be identified, but I'm almost certain they're those of Verbruggen himself."

"Any clue in the handwriting?"

DeKok smiled.

14

"No, the letters were typed. An electric machine of some kind."

"How much money was asked?"

DeKok shook his head in frustration.

"There is no question of money at all. Just a bare announcement that the baby will be kidnapped."

"In church?"

DeKok waved at the envelopes.

"Why don't you just read them," he said, irritation in his voice. Then he smiled suddenly and added: "You're getting to be as bad as me."

Vledder picked up the letters and held them against the light. There was no letterhead and there was no watermark. After Vledder read the letters, he re-folded them and replaced them in the envelopes.

"Excellent Dutch," he said.

DeKok looked up and grunted.

"Yes, excellent ... civilized ... without any grammatical errors and ... eh, totally incredible."

Vledder looked startled.

"Incredible?" he queried.

DeKok nodded with emphasis.

"Have you ever heard of a kidnapper who announced ahead of time what he was going to do ... to accommodate the police as much as possible?"

"What do you mean?"

With an angry gesture DeKok swept the letters back into the drawer. His face became a mask.

"I have the uncomfortable feeling," he said finally, slowly, "that someone is playing a macabre joke on us."

Vledder stood up.

"But why!?" exclaimed Vledder. "Frankly, I'm not too crazy

about being the butt of someone's twisted idea of a joke, especially on what's supposed to be my day off."

DeKok did not look up, nor did he react in any way to the outburst. He stared into the distance. In his mind's eye he again saw the beautiful face of the young Mrs. LaCroix.

"Why," he asked softly, "does a young woman go into shock when two hardworking civil servants, who happen to be policemen, introduce themselves?"

2

Commissaris* Buitendam, the tall, stately chief of Warmoes Street station, waved an elegant hand toward a chair in front of his desk.

"Have a seat, DeKok."

The gray sleuth shook his head.

"I'd rather stand. That way it won't take that long."

The Commissaris showed a hardening of the eyes and his hands seemed to grip the edge of the desk with more force than necessary. The dialogues between him and DeKok always were tension filled events, loaded with suspicion. DeKok was always on the alert for what he considered a curtailment of his police powers and the Commissaris always felt he had to unnecessarily probe for the information to which he felt he was entitled. Then the Commissaris released the grip on his desk and sank back in his chair with an attitude of acceptance.

"As you will," he said formally. He paused and picked up a

---

* Commissaris: a rank equivalent to Captain. There are only two ranks higher: Chief-Commissaris and Chief Constable. Each jurisdiction has only a single Chief Constable, the highest possible police rank. There is one Chief Constable for all of Amsterdam. Other ranks in the Municipal Police are: Constable, Constable First Class, Sergeant, Adjutant, Inspector, Chief-Inspector and Commissaris. Adjutants and below are equivalent to non-commissioned ranks. Inspector is a rank equivalent to 2nd Lieutenant.

pencil, looked at it and then replaced it on the desk. "I called you in for a reason, DeKok," he continued.

DeKok's face showed no emotion.

"That's why I'm here," he said.

The Commissaris coughed and cleared his throat.

"Mr. Schaap, the Judge-Advocate has ... eh, approached me. He is particularly displeased with your behavior in church, yesterday."

A fleeting glance of surprise flew across DeKok's face.

"Displeased?" he asked.

The Commissaris picked up the pencil again and as he continued he used it to emphasize his words.

"The Judge-Advocate is very much concerned about Mrs. LaCroix. They have known each other since they were children and he has been friends with the father for a long time."

"Verbruggen, the banker," murmured DeKok.

"Indeed, yes. Mr. Schaap has advised me that, if Mrs. LaCroix does not improve rapidly, he will insist that disciplinary action be taken against you."

DeKok grinned crookedly.

"Incredible ... the man is mad."

With a slap the Commissaris downed the pencil and sat up straight in his chair.

"I forbid you," he said with raised voice, "to talk about the Judge-Advocate in this manner. It is, it is ... impudent. What is more, it is insubordinate. Mr. Schaap told me that you said something to Mrs. LaCroix and she immediately went into a coma."

DeKok spread his hands in a gesture of innocence.

"I merely introduced myself, that's all. She promptly fell into an elegant swoon."

Buitendam crashed both fists down on the desk.

"That should never have happened," he yelled.

DeKok shook his head, as if to clear it.

"What?"

"That you introduced yourself."

This time DeKok raised his eyes to the ceiling, as if asking for divine intervention.

"Listen," he said in a reasonable tone of voice, "I get a call on a Sunday morning to rush over to the Wester Church to attend a baptism, because the child is supposedly to be kidnapped. Now you mean to tell me, I'm not even allowed to introduce myself to the mother?"

"Yes," said the Commissaris, "Mrs LaCroix did not know the police had been notified."

DeKok narrowed his eyes.

"Did she know her child was to be kidnapped?"

Buitendam shook his head.

"She knew nothing."

"And why was that?"

The Commissaris sighed.

"It was considered better *not* to inform her."

DeKok grinned broadly this time.

"And who," he asked, "was the idiot who figured that out?"

"Mr. Schaap ... he, eh, he wished to take into consideration the extremely delicate condition of her health and well-being."

DeKok felt himself grow angry.

"But he was in the church, this, this *investigative officer by preference*." He managed to make it sound like an insult. Then he took a deep breath and continued. "He saw me! Why did *he* not inform me? Or is this holier-than-thou, ivory-tower dweller too high and mighty to talk to a lowly Inspector?" He raised a finger in the air. "And you can tell him from *me*, that if anybody has the right instinct to protect her child, it's the mother!"

Commissaris Buitendam was just as angry by this time.

"I ... I will tell him *nothing!*" he yelled. "Especially not if it comes from you," he added maliciously.

Suddenly DeKok calmed down.

"I'd do it anyway," he said, smiling.

His chief jumped up and pointed at the door.

"OUT!" he yelled.

DeKok left.

* * *

Vledder smiled.

"Same thing again, right? Perhaps they should transfer the Commissaris to Headquarters. I don't think he'll last long enough to retire gracefully if he has to stay here with you in Warmoes Street"

DeKok rubbed the back of his neck. His anger slowly faded. His face which so often resembled that of a good-natured boxer, regained its usual cheerful expression. The beginning of a smile spread over his face. He tapped the calendar on the wall.

"With all this mess, I almost forgot that this is supposed to be the first day of Spring." He turned toward Vledder. "You called the hospital?"

"Yes."

"Well?"

"Mrs. LaCroix is recovering nicely. They want to keep her for a few more days, for observation. But then she can go home."

"What about an interrogation?"

Vledder shook his head.

"Out of the question, the doctor will not allow it. He's afraid she'll go into shock again."

DeKok nodded his understanding.

"What about the baby?"

Vledder smiled.

"Happy as a lark." He pointed at the telephone. "While you were … eh, having a dialogue with our boss, I was on the phone. I talked to the colleagues in Laren and they have nothing to report, but they promised to maintain extra patrols. After that I called Mr. Verbruggen. A woman answered and she told me the baby was just fine. She had just fed it."

"What sort of woman?"

Vledder shrugged.

"Probably someone who works for Verbruggen. She referred to him as 'Sir.' When I asked for him, she said that 'Sir' wasn't available. Apparently he left the house around quarter to seven last night and has not returned." The young man looked at his older friend. "And you know what I find strange?"

"No riddles," growled DeKok, "out with it."

"He also wasn't at the Bank."

Vledder watched with fascination as DeKok's eyebrows suddenly seemed to ripple in an impossible display. It was as if two, hairy caterpillars suddenly decided to dance on DeKok's forehead. Although Vledder had observed the phenomenon many times, he was still at a loss to explain it. DeKok himself seemed to be totally unaware of the independent nature of his eyebrows. It happened at the most unexpected moments and always seemed to stun the unwary observer.

"How do you know?" asked DeKok.

Vledder tapped the two threatening letters on his desk.

"I took these from your desk drawer. In order to definitely identify, or eliminate the finger prints, I needed Verbruggen's prints. That's why I called him, to set a time and also … to try and dig a little deeper. Somebody at the bank told me that Verbruggen wasn't there. When I insisted and asked what time he was expected, I was connected with another extension." He paused for effect. "Guess who finally came on the line?"

"Stop it," admonished DeKok. "Who?"

"Henri LaCroix."

"The son-in-law."

"Exactly. Apparently he's one of the higher-ups at the bank."

"And what did he tell you?"

"He had no idea about Verbruggen's whereabouts. He seemed surprised to learn he had not arrived yet."

DeKok rubbed his chin.

"Did you tell him that he wasn't at home, in Laren, either?"

Vledder nodded.

"Sure I did. But he seemed to dismiss that as unimportant. According to Henri, Verbruggen often did not spend the night at home."

"A mistress?"

Vledder pursed his lips. Then he grinned.

"I thought it better not to ask."

DeKok shook his head. He seemed more serious than the situation warranted.

"I don't agree with that. No doubt you felt you should be circumspect, but it's our job to be indiscreet. We're paid to ask uncomfortable questions."

"Well," answered Vledder easily, "if that becomes necessary, we can always check out his sex-life at some later date." He waved a hand in the air. "I don't think it's all that important. After all, nothing has happened. The bank boss simply decided to take a personal day ... so what?"

DeKok pulled out his lower lip and let it plop back. He repeated it several times. After a few seconds he suddenly pointed at Vledder.

"Call the hospital again and find out if Verbruggen really did visit his daughter last night. Also, try and see if the doctor will allow a short phone conversation with Mrs. LaCroix."

Vledder nodded, reaching for the phone.

His mentor started to pace up and down the busy detective room. The exercise helped him to organize his thoughts. The sudden disappearance of the bank director bothered him. His instinct, which seldom failed him, told him that he was at the beginning of a series of macabre happenings. What bothered him especially was that he knew so little. Everything was still vague ... unreachable. There was a picture, but it had no definition. Incomprehensible letters, a baptism and a bank director who did not appear at the bank. It seemed to him that there had to be a connection. But what?

He stopped in front of the window and stared out over the rooftops of Amsterdam without seeing them. From a distance he heard Vledder's voice. He paid no attention to the words, but with part of his mind he registered the emotion in the young Inspector's voice.

When Vledder replaced the receiver, DeKok turned around. Vledder looked shocked. He was pale and a thin bead of sweat formed on his upper lip.

"If Mr. Schaap hears about this," he said, "we're in for it."

"How's that?"

Vledder pointed at the phone.

"This conversation is not going to do her any good. Mrs. La-Croix was very much upset. Apparently her husband had already told her that her father had not appeared at the bank. She worried about that. Mr. Verbruggen was *always* there, he never missed a day. She could not remember an instance that he had even been late."

DeKok made an impatient gesture.

"Did he visit her last night?"

Vledder nodded.

"Yes, he was there. With her husband. But Verbruggen left early. He said he had an appointment in connection with some letters."

"Did she know about the letters, what kind of letters?"

Vledder shook his head.

"That's what's so strange. It seems to me that Mrs. LaCroix is rather easily upset. But now I don't know. When I asked her if she knew about the letters, what sort of letters they were, she became really upset. You could tell, even over the phone. 'Ask Henri,' she screamed, 'ask Henri.' Then she slammed the phone down."

* * *

The almost square room gave an impression of solid respectability. Deep, leather chairs stood out against a backdrop of polished oak wainscotting. A diffused light came through the heavily barred windows and a dark painting of a severe man in his late fifties looked down on the scene of understated wealth. DeKok studied the portrait. He recognized certain facets of the Amsterdam School of painting.

Henri LaCroix smiled politely.

"Mr. Verbruggen's grandfather," he explained, "the founder of the bank."

DeKok lowered himself into one of the easy chairs. He placed his old, decrepit little hat on the floor next to him. Then he leaned back and studied the young man with interest. He was expensively dressed in a dark-blue suit with a white shirt and a gray necktie. The black hair was combed back. The tanned skin was not obtained in a salon. He gave the impression of quiet competence, relaxed, but with alert eyes.

The gray sleuth looked at him indulgently.

24

"The disappearance of your father-in-law has, we think, taken on a more serious character. Your wife told us that he left early, last night, because of an appointment."

Henri LaCroix narrowed his eyes.

"You interrogated her?" he asked, anger in his voice.

DeKok shook his head.

"No, no, not at all. Just a short telephone conversation. That's all."

"Why?" It sounded hostile.

DeKok merely smiled.

"We just wanted to verify that Mr. Verbruggen had indeed visited her."

Henri stuck out his chin.

"You could have asked me."

DeKok nodded agreeably.

"But we were also interested to know if your wife knew about the threatening letters."

LaCroix leaned forward.

"Stella knew nothing," he said vehemently. "Absolutely nothing. After he received the letters, my father-in-law immediately contacted Mr. Schaap and *he* felt it better not to inform Stella." He looked surprised. "Surely, the Judge-Advocate told you that?" he added.

DeKok ignored the question as only he knew how to ignore things he either did not want to see, or hear, or know about. It was one of his more infuriating habits.

"Your wife told us that Mr. Verbruggen's appointment had something to do with certain letters he had received." He looked at the younger man sharply. "The threatening letters?"

LaCroix gestured helplessly.

"I don't know. I was already there when my father-in-law arrived and he must have left at least fifteen minutes before I did. I could not broach the subject with him, with Stella there, you see."

"But you assumed it?"

Henri LaCroix shrugged.

"It seems obvious," he admitted reluctantly. "I think he mentioned the word *letters* to make me aware of what he was talking about."

"Do you have any idea who he was planning to see … how was the meeting arranged?"

"I don't know."

DeKok smiled winningly as he leaned closer.

"But Mr. Verbruggen trusted you, is that right?"

LaCroix nodded assent.

"As far as business is concerned, certainly," he clarified. "But in private he is very closed. For instance, the fact that I am married to his daughter would, eh, inhibit him from discussing his sexual affairs, for instance."

"But those do exist?"

Henri nodded.

"Certainly."

"And you know about them?"

The other shook his head.

"As I told you … in certain matters he's very closed, did not confide in me, or anyone, as far as I know."

DeKok seemed to find the answer unimportant. He nodded to himself as if accepting the statement. "But you know from …" he began, and then did not pursue the line of questioning. He paused, staring at the barred windows.

"Do you have any idea who might have written those threatening letters?" he asked finally.

"No … no idea."

"Did you see them?"

"That neither."

DeKok looked openly amazed.

"But they are in connection with your child ... your child who was going to be kidnapped."

Henri LaCroix came to his feet. The questioning seemed to upset him. For a moment he stood with balled fists, then he relaxed slightly.

"I have no idea what that old codger is up to," he finally said, almost muttering the words.

"You mean Mr. Verbruggen," said DeKok sharply.

Henri sat down again and rested his arms on the sides of the chair. He lowered his head and then raised it again. There was a melancholy look in his eyes.

"He could have called me at home," he said after a long pause. "I was working at home all afternoon. He could have moved the time of the appointment. At least we would have had some time to confer, to plan. But no ... the great man preferred to work alone."

DeKok listened with interest to the bitter tone.

"I think we should list him as a missing person," suggested DeKok.

LaCroix raised his hands, as if to push the suggestion away.

"No, no," he protested. "Never ... not yet. It will reach the press and the consequences could be fatal ... for the bank," he said lamely. "I mean," he hastened to add, "You see what I mean, Managing Director disappeared ... it would harm ... a bank is primarily built on trust .... you see what it would look like?"

A phone, on a small table in a corner of the room, suddenly rang out loud. Vledder, who had been sitting next to it and had studiously kept in the background while he made copious notes, lifted the receiver as if it was the most natural thing to answer phones in somebody else's office.

"It's for you," he said to DeKok.

"What is it?" asked DeKok, making no move to take the phone. There was a resigned look on his face.

Vledder listened, then paled. Without a word he replaced the receiver.

"We've been called in," he reported hoarsely. "It's a murder case, now."

DeKok looked from LaCroix to his assistant and back again.

"Mr. Verbruggen?" he asked.

Vledder nodded.

"Yes, he's been found ... murdered."

3

Vledder manoeuvred the old police VW Beetle through the heavy traffic of Amsterdam.

"Fifty-seven horses," he muttered, "and they're all fighting each other."

Nevertheless he handled the ancient vehicle as if it was one of the latest editions of the venerable vehicle at ten times the cost. From Dam Square he took a few shortcuts and narrowly avoided a woman with a stroller in front of the BeeHive Department Store. A little later a truck blocked the narrow space along a canal. Vledder braked hard and used the horn liberally.

DeKok, who was seated next to him in his usual, relaxed pose, pushed his hat out of his eyes and looked up with mild interest.

"Take it easy," he advised. "Dead is dead. It doesn't make any difference to Mr. Verbruggen if we're a few minutes late."

Vledder made an angry gesture.

"But that truck is not supposed to park there. It's blocking all traffic."

DeKok looked through the windshield.

"Where are we going, anyway?" he asked mildly.

"Mill's Quarter."

The gray sleuth looked surprised.

"Mill's Quarter?" he asked, astonishment in his voice.

Vledder nodded, keeping one angry eye on the offending truck.

"Boven Street 387 ... an apartment."

"But that's in Amsterdam-North."

"Sure it is ... it's clearly out of our territory. But it was an express request from the Judge-Advocate. He wants *us* to look into the Verbruggen murder."

"Well," said DeKok, "will wonders never cease?" He rooted around in his pockets and found a toffee. Calmly he removed the wrapper and placed the sweet in his mouth. The empty wrapper went back in his pocket. "Mr. Schaap," he said to himself.

The truck finally moved and Vledder started the VW. He shrugged as he shifted gears.

"I don't understand it either," he admitted. "Clearly the murder should be handled by the Wadden Street station, or the Serious Crimes Unit at Headquarters. Buitendam seemed so overwhelmed," he added, "that I just didn't ask about the whys and wherefores."

DeKok chewed his toffee and nodded to himself.

"Was that him, on the phone?"

"Yes. Apparently he tried to reach us everywhere." He grinned. "Even our Commissaris knows enough not to try us on the car radio." He looked at the cunningly disguised instrument without a single ready light indicating its operational status. "Anyway," continued Vledder, "then Mr. Schaap suggested we might be at the Ysselstein Bank."

"Panic," growled DeKok in a scornful tone.

"Seems that way," agreed Vledder.

Although DeKok did not feel a single bump, or jerk, the car suddenly made some strange noises that sounded suspiciously like grinding gears. Vledder exited Prince Henry Quay and approached the Harbor Tunnel.

"You could have taken the Coen Tunnel," said DeKok, "it's shorter."

Vledder grinned at his old partner.

"Dead is dead," he mocked, "It doesn't make any difference to Mr. Verbruggen if we're a few minutes late."

DeKok placed his hat over his face and slumped back down in the seat. There was a faint smile on his face.

* * *

The apartment building was typical for that part of Amsterdam. Long rows of front doors facing a wide gallery, which is actually a continuous balcony. The gallery acts as a street with the front doors and windows of the individual apartments on one side and a view on the other side. The view was spoiled by other, similar buildings. Elevators and stairs at either end of the building led to other floors and the city street.

A young, uniformed constable guarded the door of number 387. His cap was pushed to the back of his head. When he saw Vledder and DeKok, he hastily put his cap in the proper position and straightened his tunic.

"Constable Blinker," he reported. Then he added less formally: "I'm glad you're here, sir. I hope you don't mind that I waited outside. I mean, alone with a corpse ..."

"You're the only constable on duty?"

"Yes, sir. Chief-Inspector Westerhof and Detective-Inspector Ping were here earlier, from Wadden Street Station."

"Did they leave any instructions?"

The young constable shook his head.

"No, sir. The Chief-Inspector informed the Judge-Advocate and received instruction to leave everything for you. That's what we did, but after a while they just left." There was an almost invisible twinkle in his eyes. "They seemed upset."

DeKok nodded.

"I understand. I don't like it either when somebody else is assigned to my job. I'll call them later. Has the 'herd' been called? What about the Coroner?"

"Nobody has been called, sir."

DeKok gave him a smile.

"Would you mind?" he asked.

"Not at all, sir," said the young cop. Even in this remote part of Amsterdam, DeKok was well-known and everybody on the force knew that DeKok invariably referred to the "herd," or "Thundering Herd," when he meant the small army of technical experts that always gathered at the scene of a murder.

The constable went down to his patrol car. Vledder and DeKok studied the door of the apartment. The frame seemed intact and the lock did not look as if it had been tampered with. The windows, too, showed no sign of forcible entry.

Carefully DeKok pushed against the door and entered a spacious foyer. Against one wall of decorative flagstones stood an antique, oaken cupboard. A gray raincoat hung sloppily from a wooden dowel on the side of the cupboard. Next to the cupboard, on the mosaic tiles was a hat with the white silk lining clearly visible. DeKok leaned over and read out the initials ACV.

"Albert Cornelis Verbruggen," translated Vledder. "He must have been in a hurry."

DeKok nodded. Slowly he stood up and then pushed open the inner door leading to the apartment. He saw a long, rectangular living room with modern furniture. Almost in the center, within the circle of light thrown by a pink, standing lamp, on a white carpet was the body of a man.

DeKok stood in the door opening and looked carefully at everything he could see from his position. During his long career he had confronted death many times, in many guises. And over the years he had developed almost a sixth sense, a feeling for proportions and situations ... an extra sense that immediately seemed to register disturbing influences, something out of harmony with the total picture.

Carefully he approached the body. The body was on its left side, leaning on a bent elbow. Both knees had been pulled up, as if in the foetal position.

DeKok knelt down and looked into a set of dead, gray eyes. The mouth was partially open and a narrow trail of blood showed from one corner of the mouth across the cheek. Under the chin, just below the Adam's apple and just above the starched collar he discovered a round hole ... an almost perfectly round hole, a little over a centimeter wide. Blood had stained the pearly gray necktie.

Vledder knelt down next to his partner.

"Shot?"

DeKok nodded, not responding to the question, but more as if to confirm his own observation. Then he pointed at the hole in the neck.

"There's something strange here," he said, "I believe this is an exit wound."

Vledder looked at him.

"But then, where is the entrance wound?"

DeKok did not answer, lost in his own thoughts. His attention was drawn to some small, wool fibers on the knees of the corpse's trousers. Laboriously he pushed himself up. His face was expressionless, but behind the facade his brain worked at full speed. Again he gazed around the room. He noted the position of the furniture, the expensive couch, upholstered with an expensive, white leather. He looked at the pinkish carpets on the wall and estimated their value. His gaze rested on a sad, porcelain Pierrot in a glass whatnot.

* * *

The young constable returned.

"They're on their way," he announced.

DeKok pointed at the corpse.

"Who discovered him?" he asked.

"The occupant."

"The resident of *this* apartment?"

"Yes, sir. Chief-Inspector Westerhof spoke with her briefly. I was there, but she said little. She was very upset and for now the neighbors are taking care of her. But the Chief-Inspector did tell her to be available for questioning."

DeKok grinned briefly.

"A friendly gesture by Westerhof, I'm sure." He looked around the room again and then back to the constable. "Do you have a name for the occupant? There was no name outside the door."

"Oh, yessir." DeKok watched with approval as the constable took a notebook from his chest pocket. "Her name is Carla Heeten," said the constable. "The address you know. She's twenty-seven." The constable pursed his lips in appreciation. "She's a piece," he added.

DeKok looked nonplussed.

"Eh? What's that?"

The young man grinned shamefacedly.

"You know," he said, "a piece ... a good-looking woman."

DeKok cocked his head and rubbed the back of his neck. He stared icily at the constable.

"Ah ... a piece." It sounded like a reprimand and there was

34

no doubt that the constable felt it that way.

Bram Weelen entered the room with his usual hearty manner. He placed an aluminum suitcase on a chair and shook hands with DeKok.

"You're in luck," panted the photographer. "I was in the neighborhood when the call came through." He looked at the old Inspector. "What are you doing here in North? Bit out of your territory, isn't it. You transferred to Wadden Street?"

DeKok smiled.

"No, I'm still in Warmoes Street, but this is a special ... eh, request from the Judge-Advocate."

"Oh," said Weelen, turning away and unlocking his suitcase. "Somebody important, eh?"

DeKok shrugged.

"A Bank Director," he said casually, "who only yesterday assisted in the baptism of his grandson."

Bram Weelen grunted something unintelligible and straightened up with a Hasselblad camera in his hands. He mounted a flash attachment and then addressed DeKok.

"Any special requests?"

DeKok shook his head.

"Not here. But I do want you to take photos during the autopsy." Weelen grimaced. "I am especially interested in the entrance wound." When Weelen looked a question, DeKok continued: "I think that the visible wound is an exit wound and I can't find the entrance in the position he's in."

Weelen nodded. He crouched down on one knee and took his first shot.

Vledder had discovered a drawer full of papers and was going through them. DeKok approached and tapped him on the shoulder.

"Did you find a shell?"

"No, no shells," answered Vledder. "I think it was a revolver."

"A bullet?"

Vledder shrugged.

"Possibly, I looked casually, but that carpet is so thick, you'll need special gear to find it. Nice job for the rest of the Herd," he added.

"All right, but don't forget."

"No, I'll let you know."

DeKok turned around and greeted Kruger, the fingerprint expert. Kruger, too, seemed surprised to find DeKok in Amsterdam-North.

"You're away from your usual haunts as well," commented DeKok.

"Well," said Kruger, busying himself with his accoutrements, "When I heard you were here ..." He did not finish the sentence.

"Thank you," said DeKok. Then he pointed vaguely at the room. "This may have a connection with some threatening letters I was trying to run down."

"I see," said Kruger. "Do we have him in our records, do you think?

"I don't think so," answered DeKok. His name is A.C. Verbruggen ... a Bank Director."

"Any clues?"

"Not a one."

"Well, I better cover everything, then," said Kruger.

DeKok nodded his thanks and watched silently as more and more people entered the apartment. Somebody sprayed a black outline on the pristine white carpet. Others removed pillows, looked behind wall hangings and yet others spread out over different rooms in the apartment.

Amid this apparent confusion there was a sudden lull as an old gentleman, dressed in striped trousers and frock coat which seemed to belong to a previous century, quietly entered the room. A small bag was in one hand and in his other hand he held a large, wilting Garibaldi hat. DeKok walked towards him.

"Dr. Koning," he said politely. "How good of you to come."

The old man shook hands with the old Inspector.

"No matter, DeKok," said the Coroner. I'm covering this part of town also, for a few days. My colleague had to attend a seminar, or some such nonsense." DeKok made sympathetic noises. "Nothing but foolishness," continued the Coroner, "If it was at least a medical seminar, but no, it has something to do with the EEC. About how all Coroners, all over Europe, are supposed to follow the same guidelines. Rubbish."

DeKok had a real affection and a great deal of respect for the old medical expert, but he also knew that the old man was one of the few civil servants vehemently opposed to the European Union. The old Benelux had always been good enough for the conservative doctor. Gently he took the doctor by an elbow and escorted him to the corpse.

"We presume he's dead."

It sounded frivolous and Dr. Koning looked annoyed.

"Death is no joke," he admonished.

"I am sorry, Doctor, it was not meant jokingly."

"Hm," grunted the Doctor and accepted Vledder's helping hand as he kneeled down next to the corpse. With a gentle gesture he closed the glassy eyes.

"That is better," he said. "there is nothing left for him to see on the outside." He pointed at the wound in the neck. "This is where the bullet came out," he observed.

DeKok nodded.

"I suspected it."

The Coroner, again assisted by Vledder, rose to his feet.

"He is dead," he said formally.

"Thank you, Doctor," answered DeKok, just as formally. By Dutch Law a person is not dead unless officially pronounced dead by a Coroner, or another medical doctor.

DeKok led the Coroner away from the corpse, while he motioned to two men with a stretcher who had been waiting in the door opening.

"Neck shot?" probed DeKok.

The Coroner took off his pince-nez and carefully polished it with an enormous, silk handkerchief he took out of a breast pocket. He nodded.

"During the autopsy they can determine the exact path of the shot. In any case, the killer stood behind the victim.

DeKok gave him a pensive look.

"He must have been tall."

"You mean that otherwise he could not have aimed at a down-angle?"

"Exactly."

Dr. Koning stared at his hands.

"There is another explanation."

"Yes, Doctor?"

"The victim could have been looking up."

Bram Weelen, DeKok's favorite police photographer, was packing up. While he replaced his equipment in the aluminum suitcase, he watched the two stretcher bearers place the body, now wrapped in a body bag, on the stretcher.

"You'll have your pictures tomorrow," he said to DeKok as he waved himself out the door.

DeKok grinned and raised a hand.

"Don't send them by mistake to Wadden Street," he called after the disappearing photographer.

"Warmoes Street, without fail," Weelen yelled back.

Dr. Koning nodded to the stretcher bearers as they picked up the stretcher. The two men also disappeared.

"It is strange," said Dr, Koning, turning back to DeKok, "we always seem to meet at a crossing with death."

DeKok smiled.

"It's our fate, Doctor."

DeKok stared after the old man as he followed the stretcher bearers. In his mind he went over the number of times he had witnessed the same scene. A victim of a violent crime, formless and anonymous in a black body bag, carried between two people with expressionless faces. It always made a him a little sad.

As often before he realized that he had a debt to pay ... a debt to the victim ... a debt that would remain unpaid until the murderer had been identified and apprehended.

From the corner of his eyes he saw Kruger approach.

"I found something," said the fingerprint expert.

"So soon?" asked DeKok.

For a moment Kruger looked nonplussed, then he smiled.

"No, not an identifiable print," he said, "but this. It was under the Pierrot in the whatnot."

He handed DeKok a piece of paper the size of a postcard.

DeKok read the message out loud.

"*I have called thee by thy name; thou art Mine.*"

Vledder looked up.

"The text of the baptismal service," he said.

Sometimes Vledder had a tendency to state the obvious.

4

"*I have called thee by thy name; thou art Mine.*"

DeKok read the text several times, each time with the emphasis in a different place. It was as if he were looking for a revelation. He held the paper up against the light. Then he studied the individual letters.

"Unless I'm mistaken," he said hesitantly, "it's the same paper as was used for the threatening letters." He turned toward Kruger. "It was *under* the Pierrot?"

The fingerprint expert nodded.

"I didn't see it until I lifted the statuette to examine it for prints. Perhaps part of it was sticking out, I don't know for sure. But if Bram did his job right, it must be possible to see from the pictures."

DeKok shrugged.

"Did you find anything else?"

"The maid is a slob," grinned Kruger, "and the bedroom is a favorite spot."

"How's that again?"

Kruger pointed over his shoulder.

"I found so many different prints in the bedroom, that it must have been used by at least ten couples."

DeKok laughed.

"A communal bed."

Ben Kruger grunted.

"But no children's prints."

DeKok looked around.

"I hardly expected that here."

The expert started to pack his accoutrements and closed his bags. He looked worried.

"This is a nasty case, DeKok," he said earnestly. "I don't know how, but it smells. You'll have your hands full, if I'm any judge." He walked toward the door. "I'll sort out the prints and let you know."

DeKok waved goodbye.

Vledder took the paper with the text from DeKok's hand and sniffed it.

"No perfume," he concluded. "Who could have put it there … and why?"

DeKok did not answer the question, but made a comment.

"It's about time we collect Carla Heeten from the neighbors and have a heart-to-heart talk."

Vledder hesitated for a moment and remained in front of DeKok, willing him to look at his partner.

"The text … by whom … why?"

DeKok's face became a mask.

"By somebody," he said grimly, "who wanted to make sure that we make a connection betwcen the killing and the ceremony at Wester Church."

* * *

She entered slowly. An expensive fur coat slid from her shoulders. Vledder leaned forward and placed the coat over his arm. There was fear in the pale face of Carla Heeten. Her large, blue eyes roamed around the room and came to rest on the carpet, where the outline of Verbruggen's body was clearly visible. Gently Vledder pushed her into the room.

DeKok approached. There was a faint, friendly smile on his face.

"My name is DeKok," he said, "DeKok with kay-oh-kay." He pointed at Vledder. "You have already met my colleague, Vledder."

She nodded slowly and took DeKok's outstretched hand. Then she shook her head. "I didn't do it," she said tonelessly, "I didn't do it."

DeKok merely smiled and led her to an easy chair.

"Please sit down," he said in a fatherly tone. "You live here?"

Her tongue moistened her lips.

"This is my apartment."

"How long have you lived here?"

"Almost five years."

DeKok pointed at the furniture, the expensive wall hangings.

"The decor ... your own concept?"

Carla Heeten avoided his eyes.

"My friend."

"He lives here too?"

She shook her head.

"I live alone."

"Your profession?"

She did not answer.

"Your profession?" repeated DeKok in a friendly tone of voice.

"I am ... eh, a call-girl."

DeKok nodded his understanding.

"And Mr. Verbruggen was a client?"

She stood up and looked wildly around, as if trying to escape.

"I ... I mean, he did not visit me, I mean, I didn't know. I had no idea he'd be coming here."

"But you knew him?"

"Yes."

"In your capacity as a call-girl?"

Slowly she sank back into the chair.

"Albert ... Mr. Verbruggen has been visiting me for years. We got along fine together. I got to know him through Jean-Paul Dervoor. One day he brought him along. That was more than a week after his wife had left him."

"And you consoled him?"

Carla Heeten looked insulted.

"I don't know if you mean that mockingly, but Albert was due for some understanding and feminine tenderness. His wife never appreciated his feeling ... his real feelings. She simply did not understand him."

DeKok nodded to himself.

"Dervoor," he said finally, "Jean-Paul Dervoor ... Director of Electronics International?"

A smile almost appeared on her face. She pulled her shoulders back and pushed her chest out.

"I have a large and ... an influential clientele."

DeKok cocked his head at her. He had heard the vague hint of a threat in her voice.

"Albert ... Mr. Verbruggen," he continued, "suddenly came here, unannounced, to visit you?"

Carla shook her head. The blonde hair formed a brief halo.

"He did not come in. I mean ... I was not here. I just found him a few hours ago, when I came home."

She pointed at the outline on the floor.

"He was right there, on his side. I never doubted it for a moment. I could see from the eyes that he was dead."

"And then you immediately called the police?"

She lowered her head.

"No," she whispered, "first I called my friend."

DeKok looked surprised.

"But why?"

"It is never good for someone's reputation ... the family especially ... I mean, when a man is found dead in the apartment of a call-girl ..." She did not finish the sentence, but looked up at the Inspector. "I did not want to do anything thoughtless, to create a scandal ... you know what I mean?"

DeKok nodded soothingly.

"Apart from your friend, did you call anyone else?"

"No."

DeKok rubbed the back of his neck.

"Where were you yesterday ... Sunday?"

"With my friend. I spend every week-end with him. I only have visitors during the week. That's what this apartment is for."

"And Mr, Verbruggen knew this?"

"Certainly."

"Yet ... he came on a Sunday when he knew you would not be here. Why?"

Carla spread her hands wide.

"I don't know." She sounded annoyed. "I have no idea what was on his mind."

"How did he get in?"

She sighed.

"Albert has a key. All my ... eh, better clients have a key."

"Aren't you afraid of surprises?"

She shook her head.

"That doesn't bother me. They can even give the key ... as long as it is paid for ... they can even lend the key to friends, or relations."

"And that happens?"

"Sometimes."

DeKok paused. Meanwhile he continued to watch her intently. The young constable had been right. Carla Heeten was a beautiful woman. Long, gold-blonde hair cascaded down to her shoulders. Her face was delicately molded and the ivory skin looked healthy with a glow of its own. Even more expressive than the large, blue eyes were the full, sensual lips, accentuated with a dark, red lipstick. As far as DeKok could determine, it was her only make-up. Shamelessly he studied the rest of her figure.

"An extremely desirable woman," he muttered, "as if created to please men."

A dark fire lit up her eyes.

"I will put in a complaint about you," she said sharply. "Your remarks are downright insulting."

With a shock DeKok realized he had spoken his thoughts aloud. But he smiled amiably.

"I meant it as a compliment," he said.

Her cheeks became red. It only increased her attractiveness.

"You'll hear more about this. I know a Judge-Adv ..."

Suddenly she stopped.

DeKok gave her a broad grin.

"Can you type?"

She snorted. Even that gesture was attractive.

"Typing ... yes, I learned it some time ago."

"When you still had hopes of a more ... eh, respectable career?"

Carla Heeten reacted angrily.

"Respectable!" she yelled suddenly, "Respectable!" she repeated with scorn in her voice. "Who is respectable these days? The highly placed gentlemen who visit me regularly?"

DeKok showed no emotion.

"What's the name of your friend?"

"Jimmy ... Jimmy Munk."

DeKok glanced briefly at Vledder.

"Jimmy Munk," continued DeKok. "Jimmy Munk ... doesn't he have a record? A number of convictions for blackmail, I think."

She jumped up. She had clearly lost any shred of self-control. She made fists and her body trembled.

"It wasn't Jimmy." Her voice cracked. "Jimmy doesn't have anything to do with it. You can't blame him. Not this time! Jimmy was with me!"

* * *

As they drove away from Mill's Quarter it was getting dark and the rain increased. Vledder switched on the radio and listened to the traffic police band. It was crowded with reports of fender benders and more serious accidents. DeKok turned off the unit. The noise bothered him and he wanted to think.

Vledder broke in on his pondering.

"You were not exactly polite, were you?"

"Perhaps not, but I wanted her to talk. Besides, there was no reason to be polite to her."

"What!? Don't tell me that you look down on call-girls!"

DeKok looked at his young partner with astonishment.

"What did you say? Look down ... No, of course not. No, it was something else. When I looked at her, I suddenly realized that I had seen her before."

"Where?"

"At the station house. In Warmoes Street."

"As a suspect?"

DeKok shook his head.

"No, she was a witness in a case where her friend played a rather ambiguous part."

"Do you know this Jimmy Munk?"

"I know of him. I have never had a case involving him. But I have seen him ... and Carla in the detective room when they were being interrogated by colleagues."

"How does Jimmy operate?"

"Well, with Carla as bait, he gets influential people in compromising situations."

"Tried and true," commented Vledder.

"Blackmail," agreed DeKok.

They finally reached the station house and Vledder parked in front. The rain had increased even more and DeKok raised the collar of his raincoat and pressed his little hat deeper in his eyes.

There seemed to be a small riot in front of the door. An older man stood among some curiosity seekers. The old man was dressed in only a pair of trousers and a sodden shirt. He was drunk. Repeatedly he tried to enter the station, but two constables kept pushing him back.

When the old man saw DeKok he fell down on his knees. Pleadingly the old man raised his hands to DeKok.

"Mr. DeKok ... they picked up little Billy."

"Your son."

"Yes. They say he cut someone. But Billy ain't that way. You know him, don't you, Mr. DeKok? The boy has never harmed anyone. He don't even got a knife."

Together with Vledder, DeKok lifted the old man to his feet.

"Go home, Bert," he said calmly. "I'll take a look at Billy." Then he turned to the constables. "Take him home. He lives along the canal, just around the corner, a few blocks."

The two men nodded agreeably and took Bert between them. The Inspectors entered the station house. The Watch Commander, Meindert Post, stood behind the counter that separated the public part of the lobby from the rest of the building. DeKok leaned his elbows on the railing.

"Did you lock up Billy Vlerk?"

Meindert Post nodded.

"A few hours ago he stabbed a Swede in *The Safe Harbor*. They were fighting over a girl. The victim has been taken to Wilhelmina Hospital. I am still waiting on a report, but the damage seems to be minor."

DeKok nodded toward the front door.

"Bert wanted to get in."

The Watch Commander grinned.

"Drunk as a Templar. He's been here at least five times to tell me that Billy didn't do it. It finally started to annoy me. That's when I put him outside."

Post consulted his Log Book. Then he grabbed a piece of paper and scribbled a number.

"You're supposed to call this number," he said.

DeKok gave the scrap of paper to Vledder.

"Do you mind calling? I'm going to look in on Billy."

DeKok waddled down the stairs to the cell block. He opened the hatch in number three.

"Your father is worried," he called into the cell.

A pale face with a smile of recognition appeared on the other side of the door.

"Hello, Mr. DeKok," said Billy Vlerk. He laughed shyly. "If you see the old man, tell him not to worry. That guy was just asking for it."

"Was there a knife, Billy?"

"Sure, Mr. DeKok, but it was *his* knife. I took it away from him," Billy added proudly.

"Well, then it *could* be self-defense. But you should have thrown the knife away, after you took it off him. This will just not do, Billy. Fighting is one thing, but I don't want you to use a knife, ever."

"Honest, Mr. DeKok, I wasn't going to, but ... it just happened."

"Yes, it usually happens when one has a knife handy. I'll see what I can do for you, but no more fighting, ever. The next time you're in a fight, I'll personally see to it you're going away for a long time and ... you'll be banished from the Quarter for life."

"Gee, Mr. DeKok, I live with me old man, right here in the Quarter. What am I going to do?"

"Simple, Billy, no more fighting."

"OK, Mr. DeKok, I promise. Will you tell my father?"

"Yes, I'll reassure him."

"Thank you, Mr. DeKok."

The gray sleuth nodded and closed the hatch. Billy went back to his bunk, assured that his father would be calmed, that a good defense lawyer would be appointed and above all, certain that he would never, ever be able to even visit the Red Light District if he broke his promise to DeKok. Billy considered it a new beginning. For DeKok it was just one more small interlude in his ongoing battle to maintain Law and Order. He never seemed to realize that these little talks with a variety of culprits sometimes did more to fight crime than all the jail sentences and rehabilitation programs together.

Vledder met him in the corridor. He looked serious and DeKok asked what was the matter.

"Stella LaCroix has disappeared," said Vledder.

"Disappeared?"

"Yes," nodded Vledder. "She walked away from the hospital."

"Home?"

"No."

"To Laren, to her father's house?

"No, although she's been there."

"All right, tell me what happened."

"She took the baby out of the crib and then drove off with the baby in her father's Bentley ... car," added Vledder, knowing that DeKok did not know a Bentley from a VW.

"Where did she go?"

"That's the problem," said Vledder. Henri LaCroix has called everybody he could think of. He's at his wit's end. There is no trace of Stella."

5

They left the corridor and with tired steps they climbed the stairs to the detective room. DeKok threw his wet raincoat over his right shoulder and shoved his hat back on his head. He was tired, exhausted. The way things were going was not to his liking. There was a thread, he was certain, but he could not find the beginning, or the end. There had to be a connection. In his mind he went over the various items: the strange threatening letters, the baptism, then the violent death of Verbruggen and now the sudden flight of Stella with her baby. Had she indeed fled? If so ... because of what ... because of whom?

A young woman screamed and banged on the door of her cell. Vledder grimaced.

"It's bad enough to have to lock up men, but there is something obscene about having to lock up women," he commented.

DeKok did not react. His thoughts were miles away.

"The phone number Meindert gave us is that of Henri La-Crois?"

Vledder nodded.

"The hospital contacted him originally that his wife had dressed and disappeared. She was seen leaving through the Helmer Street gate and Henri thought she was coming home."

"To Churchill Lane?"

"Yes. But when she did not show up in a reasonable amount of time he became worried and called Laren. The housekeeper told him that she had left less than fifteen minutes earlier."

"How?" asked DeKok.

"What do you mean?"

"Apart from the baby, did she take anything else, clothes, a suitcase, whatever?"

Vledder looked embarrassed.

"I never asked."

They entered the detective room. DeKok threw his wet raincoat and just as sodden hat on an empty table. Vledder switched on his computer and industriously transferred his many notes from his notebook to the computer. For a while the only sound was the soft clacking of the keyboard. DeKok looked on. He did not believe in computers. He depended on his notebook, his memory and his experience. But he always insisted that the notebook was the most important part of a cop's equipment. But, he admitted to himself, since Vledder had joined him as partner, his life had become a lot easier. The young inspector had developed his own program and in the shortest possible time could produce almost any type of report about ongoing cases from the information stored in the machine. It certainly made life easier with the bureaucracy, thought DeKok.

He fished around in his pockets and after a while he found the scrap of paper with the Bible text. He stared at it for a while.

"Do you have the description of that car?" DeKok asked suddenly.

Vledder knew him well enough to be able to respond immediately. A few keystrokes were all that was required.

"A dark-brown Bentley," he read from the screen. "License tag 62-JV-08. There is a slight dent on the front fender, above the headlights. I already put an APB in the system, with copies to the border crossings."

"Fine," smiled DeKok, "but I did not know the border crossings were still manned."

"Oh, yes," answered Vledder. "Skeleton crews, mostly, and they hardly ever stop anyone anymore ... but they're still there. Despite the EEC, I guess it'll take time to phase them out altogether."

"What is a Bentley?" asked DeKok.

"Looks a bit like a Rolls-Royce," answered Vledder and then added for DeKok's benefit: "Large, boxy car, made in England."

"Oh, yes," smiled DeKok. "Well, at least it is a noticeable car and we have some hope of finding her. I'm a bit worried that we'll find her with a bullet in her, as well." He paused. "Did Stella know about her father's death?" he asked.

Vledder nodded, again consulting his screen.

"Henri told her during visiting hours at the hospital. Naturally he was as circumspect as possible. The doctor was there, too."

"And what was her reaction?"

"According to Henri, reasonably good. No hysterics, or anything like that."

DeKok pulled out his lower lip, while Vledder rested his hands easily on the keyboard. Both men were comfortable with the routine. They asked each other questions, not just for information, but also to set the facts firmer in their minds. But then, thought Vledder, DeKok almost always refuses to read reports.

"The death of her father," said DeKok after a long silence, "must have been the trigger for her to leave the hospital and take off with her child."

"You think so?"

"It's the only thing I can think of."

Vledder looked shocked.

"But that would mean that she's aware of, or suspects she knows, the background to the whole affair. She must have some idea about what led to Verbruggen's killing."

DeKok nodded to himself and listened for a while to the noise made by a defective ballast in the fluorescent light overhead. Vledder stood on his desk and whacked it a few times. The noise became less and one additional tube came on.

"Do you have the phone number in Laren?" asked DeKok suddenly.

Vledder climbed down.

"I do," he said as he again touched his keyboard.

DeKok pointed at the phone.

"Call the housekeeper and ask for the address of Mrs. Verbruggen."

Vledder's hand was already on the phone, but he looked confused.

"Mrs. Verbruggen?" he asked.

DeKok nodded quietly.

"Yes, Mrs. Verbruggen," he repeated. "At one time she gave her husband a daughter, remember?"

Vledder obtained the information and when he saw DeKok pull on his coat, he looked at the clock.

"But, it's past ten."

"It's never too late, my boy, for a condolence visit."

* * *

"Where is the address?" asked DeKok, after they had gotten into the car.

Vledder did not answer. All his attention was needed to extricate the vehicle from Warmoes Street and through the rest of the busy Red Light District. As usual the Quarter was busy.

"Well?" repeated DeKok, oblivious to the traffic.

Vledder grabbed in a side pocket and gave his partner a scrap of paper. DeKok pushed the switch for the dome light and read Vledder's note.

"Louise Kolfs," he read out loud. "Herb Way 765 in Dovecote. He pushed the note back into Vledder's pocket.

"Louise Kolfs?" he wondered.

Vledder grinned.

"Got you there, haven't I? She used to be Mrs. Verbruggen. At one time she gave her husband a daughter, remember?" he mocked.

DeKok smiled.

"And now she's Louise Kolfs."

"No, now she's Louise Kolfs *again*. She assumed her maiden name immediately after the divorce."

DeKok switched off the dome light.

"Is that what the housekeeper said? Immediately?" When Vledder nodded, he continued. "Did she have anything else to say?"

"It was almost impossible to get a coherent sentence out of her. What with everything the last few days, she's completely, as she put it, outside her nerves. She carried on about 'poor Mr. Verbruggen' and that naughty girl who stole her baby."

"Outside her nerves," laughed DeKok, "I like that, very expressive. But did she really call Stella a *naughty girl?*"

The younger man grinned.

"I did not pursue it. I was far too happy to get the address."

DeKok nodded agreement.

"Still," he said after some thought, "it won't hurt to have a little talk with her, one of these days. For instance," he continued, "I'd like to know how much luggage Stella took with her."

Vledder slapped his own head.

"How stupid," he groaned, "that's the second time I forgot to ask."

DeKok did not say anything, but slid comfortably down into the seat, while he slowly unwrapped a stick of chewing gum. He loved these moments. They reminded him of the time when he had placed his own first steps on the slippery path of law enforcement. He rolled the wrapper into a tiny ball and flipped it into the ashtray. How many times, he reflected, had he slipped up himself? And not every mistake had been made in his early days, either. He remembered some painful incidents from the recent past.

* * *

Herb Way in Dovecote turned out to be a long, quiet lane with large houses with driveways and some expensive condominiums. About fifty yards beyond number 765 Vledder parked the old VW on the side of the road and together they sauntered back to the address.

The garden was bordered by railroad ties, constructed in intricate terraces full of flowers and exotic plants. Yellow narcissus encircled a tall pine tree. DeKok passed the tree and looked up. There was still a light on the second floor. He looked at the nameplate next to the doorbell and pushed. After some time "Who is there?" sounded from a small loudspeaker above the doorbell. DeKok bowed into the direction of the speaker and took off his hat out of habit.

"My name is DeKok," he said in a friendly tone of voice. "DeKok, with kay-oh-kay. Next to me is my colleague, Vledder. We're police officers attached to Warmoes Street Station."

"Detectives?"

There was suspicion and a hint of surprise in the female voice that sounded back.

"We would like to talk to you."

"What about?"

DeKok laughed softly.

"The subject matter is hardly appropriate for an impersonal chat with a ... eh, a wall."

There was silence.

"You are right," said the voice. "I'll come down."

It took a few minutes. Then the light in the hall went on and a woman opened the door. DeKok estimated her age to be in the late forties. She was tall, slender and very dignified. She wore black slacks and a black sweater. She cocked her head at the two men and gave them a condescending smile.

"Please excuse me for being careful," she said without a hint of regret, "but the hour is late."

DeKok shook his head.

"Not at all, not at all," he assured her. Then, more briskly: "You are Ms. Kolfs?"

"Yes."

"Divorced from Albert Verbruggen?"

"Indeed."

DeKok looked serious.

"You would probably have held it against us, if we had come at a different time."

She looked at him for several seconds. Then she seemed to have come to a conclusion and stepped aside, holding the door open. After she had closed the door behind the Inspectors, she led the way down a tiled hall to a wooden staircase. She smiled an apology.

"One of the problems with this type of housing," she explained, "is that one is always forced to go either up, or down."

The living room on the second floor was tastefully and cozily arranged. Some very fine landscapes decorated the walls and four easy chairs faced an open hearth of red brick.

Without waiting for an invitation, DeKok lowered himself with a deep sigh into one of the chairs, while he placed his decrepit hat on the floor next to him. When Vledder and Louise Kolfs had seated themselves as well, he stood up again. He inclined his head toward the woman.

"It is my sad duty," he said, "to tell you that your ex-husband has ... passed away."

She looked up at him.

"Albert?"

DeKok nodded slowly.

"He was found this afternoon. Your ex-husband did not die a natural death. He was murdered."

She folded her hands in her lap.

"Murdered," she repeated without any visible expression.

DeKok allowed himself to sink down into the chair again.

"The Judge-Advocate, Mr. Schaap, has given us the responsibility for the investigation."

She looked at him sharply.

"What has Jules to do with all this?"

DeKok rubbed the bridge of his nose with an outstretched finger, Then he looked at it for a while as if he had never seen it before.

"Who is Jules?" he asked.

Ms. Kolfs made a sweeping movement with her hand, as if to wipe out some unseen irritation.

"Jules ... Jules Schaap*," she snorted, contempt in her face and in her tone. "Some man ... a wolf in sheep's clothing."

"Forgive me," explained DeKok. "As you know, we have a number of Judges-Advocate. They're as proliferate as District At-

---

*Schaap is the Dutch word for sheep.

60

torneys in the United States and serve the same type of function. We do not always know them by first and last name." He paused. "But apparently you do?" he added.

She smiled wanly.

"Yes, I knew that whole clique surrounding my husband."

DeKok studied his fingertips.

"That sounds ... eh, not nice," he said. He gave her a searching look. "I mean, the word *clique* has unpleasant connotations."

Louise Kolfs shook her head.

"It's the only word that fits. My husband often flirted with criminal activities and the people he surrounded himself with, were of the same shady type."

"Including a Judge-Advocate?"

"Why not?" she asked tiredly. "Just another facade, a mask ... just like my husband ... Managing Director of the oh, so trustworthy Ysselstein Bank."

DeKok rubbed the back of his neck. Although he understood the things Ms. Kolfs said, the meaning behind the words escaped him.

"You seem ... I mean, the death of your husband doesn't seem to affect you very much," said DeKok.

Again she folded her hands in her lap.

"At this moment I feel nothing ... no sorrow, nothing. I'm just numb. Perhaps there will be a reaction later. After all, I was married to him for almost twenty years. And I *did* love him." She fell silent and the two Inspectors respected that. "But," she said after a long pause, "in my opinion he died more than seven years ago."

"When you divorced him?"

She bowed her head.

"Yes, all at once the limit had been reached. I simply could not stand it any longer. Albert didn't have any conscience, he was

… amoral. You do not normally notice that at first, from one day to the next. It's a slow process of recognition, of becoming aware. It takes years."

Again there was a long silence. Ms. Kolfs seemed withdrawn into her own thoughts. Her face was expressionless as she stared someplace over DeKok's head.

* * *

DeKok took the opportunity to study her carefully. She was not a bad-looking woman, he concluded. On the contrary. The years had hardly touched her figure. The skin was still vital and could have belonged to a younger woman. There were some lines around the mouth and in the corners of the eyes. In her hair, the color and shape of the eyes, he recognized the mother of Stella LaCroix.

He coughed discreetly to get her attention.

"You daughter, Stella, sided with your husband?"

This brought her back to reality.

"Stella," she whispered, "Stella blamed me for wanting to divorce Albert."

"Why?"

There was a sad smile on her face.

"Stella has her own principles. As far as that is concerned, she resembles her father. 'You have lived very comfortably for almost twenty years,' she said, 'although you knew his income was the result of shady practices.' You see, I remember her words exactly. She thought it was cowardly and dishonest to abandon him after all that time."

"So, she did not join you?"

"No, she stayed in Laren, with Albert."

"And married Henri LaCroix."

62

Again she smiled sadly.

"I met him a few times, you know," she mused. "Stella brought him over to get acquainted. I tried, but I could not bring myself to feel any sympathy for the boy. As a matter of fact, I was against the marriage. But my husband was very pleased with Henri and wouldn't hear a bad word about him."

"What were your objections?"

Ms. Kolfs plucked at the hem of her sweater.

"I wanted to spare her the kind of life I had led."

"You mean that LaCroix is just as callous and ... eh, shady as your husband?"

She shook her head.

"No, not callous exactly, not like Albert. But he is driven by a compelling desire to climb as high as possible in social circles. It is a sort of sickness, almost. He craves public respect. He's a social climber of the worst kind. He'll sacrifice anything to achieve his goals. Anything and anybody," she repeated.

"Even Stella?"

"Yes, he'd even sacrifice Stella."

At that moment the conversation was interrupted by the entrance of a young man, who entered the room. The man looked athletic and was dressed in a blue jogging suit. Just inside the door he stopped, surprise in his eyes. Ms. Kolfs stood up and stretched out a hand to the young man.

"This is Marius ... my son."

She walked toward her son and took his arm.

"These two gentlemen are from the police."

"Detectives?"

"That's right," said Ms. Kolfs brightly. "They're involved with an investigation. Your father has been murdered."

For just a moment the man seemed bewildered. But the expression on his face changed quickly. There was an angry look on his face when he spoke.

"Murdered," he said, grinning maliciously. "What took them so long?"

Ms. Kolfs was shocked.

"Marius!"

Marius took a step forward.

"God knows, they should have killed him seven years ago."

6

It was raining steadily as DeKok walked from the station house to a nearby bar. Vledder was at the autopsy and had not returned yet. To kill the time, DeKok went into a nearby bar to get a cup of coffee. From his vantage point near the window, he could just see the entrance to the police station and he settled down comfortably.

Suddenly a man appeared at his table. The man was of indeterminate age. He wore an old-fashioned suit with a dark-blue waistcoat. The colors combined pleasingly with the gray at his temples. He must have been in the bar for some time, because his friendly face showed the specific red that the Dutch *jenever**   usually painted on the faces of its imbibers.

"Amsterdam is at its most beautiful when it rains," declared the man.

DeKok looked up with a non-committal face. He happened to agree with the man, but he was curious to see what would happen next.

"Amsterdam is at its most beautiful when it rains," insisted the man, as if DeKok had answered in the negative. Without wait-

---

*Jenever is the Dutch national drink, made from juniper berries. Often (erronously) referred to as "schnapps." Gin is the result of the inability of the British to duplicate the process in the time of William and Mary.—transl.

65

ing for an invitation the man sat down heavily.

"Exactly," he said, as if DeKok had agreed to his statement. "When the town is covered by gray, low-hanging clouds ... when the facades are being mirrored in the wet pavement ... then, yes then, Amsterdam *shines*!"

To emphasize his words, He banged on the table. "Most cities," he continued, "cannot do without the sun. Take Rome, for instance ... or Paris. When the sun is shining ... magnificent cities. But when it rains ..." He paused as if the make sure that DeKok understood the failing of the foreign cities under those conditions. "Color, he went on, color determines their beauty. But in Amsterdam it's different. Amsterdam is colorful in black and white."

He waved at the barkeeper.

"One more and one for this gentleman," he ordered.

DeKok hastily assured him that coffee would be just fine.

The man smiled indulgently at DeKok.

"Coffee, then," he said in the tone of one bowing to the unreasonable demand of a child. Then he stared out of the window.

"It's raining cats and dogs ... no fit weather for man or beast." He sipped from his glass. "Do you know," he asked suddenly, "who founded Rome?"

"Romulus and Remus," answered DeKok slowly, his mind elsewhere.

"Exactly." The man placed a hand on DeKok's arm. "That's right ... twins ... abandoned and nursed by a wolf."

His friendly face became somber. DeKok merely nodded.

"Sad, isn't it?" asked the man. "Poor foundlings ... imagine, if you will. Two infants, crying, with small hands groping for the warm bosom of their mother. And suddenly, there's a she-wolf, she sniffs a little and ... hoopla ... those poor kids get a hairy nipple in their little mouths." He shook his head dejectedly. "I got nothing against wolves, you know. You understand, I'm all for the environment. But you have to admit ... Romulus and Remus ... how could that ever grow up to be fine, upstanding citizens ... and what about *their* offspring? Grandma was a wolf. Nice thought."

DeKok looked at the man with large eyes, wondering whether, or not, he was having his leg pulled. But the friendly face across the table was earnest and thoughtful. He waved for another drink.

"Do you know how Amsterdam came about?" he asked suddenly. "It's more than seven hundred years ... you knew that?"

DeKok, who probably knew more about Amsterdam's history than anyone alive, shook his head.

The man put a finger in his glass of *jenever* and with a wet finger he painted a wiggly snake on the table top.

"Look," he explained, "that's the Amstel River. And over here was the IJ*, or rather, the Zuyder Zee," he made a gesture as if throwing something away. Apparently the Zuyder Zee was of less importance. "Well," he went on, "you know where the Willem Locks are, don't you, that give access to what was the Zuyder Zee ... Ijssel Lake, now? But no matter, those locks came later ... much later."

He again dipped his finger in his drink.

"The Amstel," he pointed, "had no bridges, either, at that time. No bridges at all, No Berlage Bridge, no Blue Bridge, no Skinny Bridge ... nothing. Just ... water."

He licked his dry lips and suddenly tossed off his drink. He smacked his lips and waved for another drink.

"Well," he said to DeKok who was now totally absorbed by the man's tale. The man nodded approval at this obvious interest.

---

*IJ is the name of a small river that used to connect Amsterdam to the Zuyder Zee. Currently the name is applied to the harbor area.—transl.

"Well," he said again, "it so happens that on one bank of the Amstel there lived a fisherman's family and they had a son. On the other bank was a farmer's family and they had a daughter. Those two loved each other."

"Sure, that's possible," said DeKok, seduced by the story.

The man nodded gratefully.

"Now, there were boats that could be used to sail from one bank to the other, but that wasn't all that easy, you see, what with the currents and the tides. It was not unusual for someone to drown, you see."

DeKok looked a question, genuinely wondering where the story was going.

"Well," said the man, "it's obvious, isn't it?"

"No," said DeKok.

"Because those two wanted to be together, they thought of something. Whenever they had a moment, they both, each from his, or her, own bank, threw stones and clay in the water. You understand? Always stones and clay."

He smiled triumphantly.

"That's how the *dam* in Amsterdam came about. The *dam* in the Amstel ... Amstel*dam*, Amsteler*dam* and finally *Amsterdam*."

He fell silent and stared dreamily into his empty glass.

"You see the difference between here and Rome?" he asked after a long silence. "No wolves here, no abandoned children. Amsterdam was born out of love."

DeKok shook his head. Just then he saw Vledder enter the station house. He patted the man on the shoulder.

"Thank you," said DeKok as he left the bar.

* * *

"How was the autopsy?"

Vledder, who usually got stuck with that detail, shrugged his shoulders.

"Gruesome," he growled, "as always. But other than that, nothing special. Dr. Rusteloos finished in less than seventy-five minutes. He did find the path of the bullet, of course. The bullet entered through the spine, snapped the spinal cord and exited from the throat. Death was instantaneous."

"When is the funeral?"

"Tomorrow morning at eleven."

"Where?"

"Sorrow Field along the Amstel."

"You want to go?"

"Do I have to?"

DeKok grinned. He knew that Vledder disliked attending funerals, but the Law required a police officer present at the funerals of all bodies that had been subjected to an autopsy. And especially in the case of violent death. One of the duties of such an officer was to inspect the seals on the coffin, to make sure the body had not been tampered with after it was placed in the casket.

"Well, I think it's important and ... I don't want to go. Take Bram Weelen with you. I want a picture of everyone who attends."

"Why?"

Suddenly DeKok slammed his desk. Several detectives and a few suspects at desks in other parts of the room, looked up. Most of them simply shrugged. They were used to outbursts from DeKok's corner of the room.

"Because I don't know what's happening," said DeKok, a bit calmer. "We've been on this case for several days and what have we got?" He shook his had sadly. "Nothing, a big fat zero. I just met the Commissaris a few moments ago in the hall. He asked if there had been any developments. Mr. Schaap was so very interested."

Vledder glanced in his direction as he momentarily rested his fingers on the keyboard. As usual he was transferring all his information and notes to the computer.

"What did you say?"

DeKok gave him a crooked smile.

"I asked him," said DeKok, obviously savoring the memory, "why Mr. Schaap had led his friend Verbruggen to his death."

"You didn't!"

"Oh yes, I did," answered DeKok. "I think that Mr. Schaap knew all about Verbruggen's appointment in Mill's Quarter."

"How?"

"Very simple, really. Verbruggen told him. Just think a moment. Verbruggen gets threatening letters that his grandson is going to be kidnapped during the baptismal ceremony. What does he do? Does he go to the police? No! He contacts our beloved Judge-Advocate, who contacts Commissaris Buitendam, who finally gets to us. Well, in connection with these same threatening letters Verbruggen is invited to visit the apartment of Carla Heeten. Surely it's obvious that before he took such a step he checked with his friend, Mr. Schaap."

Vledder nodded thoughtfully.

"Yes, if you look at it that way, it's obvious. Do you think Schaap had a hand in the murder? Was an accomplice?"

DeKok shook his head.

"I haven't thought it out that far. But no, I don't think so. But it is entirely within the realm of possibilities that he advised Verbruggen to keep the appointment."

"But in that case, why he didn't he tell us about it?"

DeKok raised an admonishing finger.

"Now that Verbruggen has been found dead in that apartment ..."

"He's ashamed of his advice," completed Vledder.

DeKok smiled.

"Exactly. And that explains at the same time my rather bold remarks to the Commissaris. I'm sure that Buitendam will report the conversation to Schaap. Perhaps I can force Schaap to let us in on some things. I'm sure he knows more than he's telling."

Vledder shook his head in puzzlement.

"But that is just too crazy. According to the Law, the Judge-Advocate is ultimately responsible for the investigation. We're just his arms and legs, so to speak. But that also means that the Judge-Advocate, whichever of them is in charge, cannot withhold information from the investigating officers in the field."

"Perhaps," mused DeKok, "perhaps he doesn't want the perpetrator caught."

He stood up and went to the peg where his coat was hung. He slipped it on and placed his little hat squarely on top of his head.

"Now, where are you going?" Vledder wanted to know.

DeKok smiled broadly.

"Mens sana non potent vivere in corporo secco."

"What!?"

"What's the matter, my boy, forgot all your Latin? It means: *A healthy soul cannot live in a dry body.*"

"Aha," said Vledder. "We're going to Little Lowee for an inspirational glass of cognac."

"Indeed," said DeKok in a lugubrious voice.

* * *

They walked from the Warmoes Street toward Little Lowee's bar. They passed the usual tourists, sailors and other interested parties that daily, and nightly, crowd Amsterdam's Red Light District.

Apart from a tourist attraction, Amsterdam is also a busy harbor town. Ships come and go and are loaded and unloaded at all hours of the day and night. To the crews Amsterdam is a favorite liberty port and the Quarter is always happy to oblige.

Vledder and DeKok eyed the familiar atmosphere. In the distance of a single block, more than a dozen different languages could be heard and the aroma from as many different ethnic kitchens intermingled with the smell of stale beer and hard liquor.

Peep shows, sex theaters and strip clubs filled in the spaces between bars and in the side streets the prostitutes were on display in their individual windows. It was a scene of abandon and sexual excess, yet the average tourist was safer here, than in most quite residential streets. The Quarter policed itself and when they failed, DeKok and his colleagues stepped in.

DeKok looked around and absorbed the spectacle in which he had fought crime for more than a quarter century. It was always different and also, sadly, always the same. Unlike most, he identified individuals, rather than a mob. From time to time a prostitute, or a more shady character of the underworld would call out a greeting. Some greetings he acknowledged and some he ignored. He never acknowledged a pimp in any way.

He looked aside at Vledder.

"Any news about Stella?"

"No," said Vledder, "it's a real mystery. Those two seem to have disappeared from the face of the earth. Henri, too, hasn't heard from his wife. The last time anyone saw her, was when the housekeeper saw the car drive away." He laughed sheepishly. "But this time, when I talked to Henri, I remembered to ask about the luggage."

"And?"

"Just a small suitcase with some underwear, make-up stuff and clothes for the baby."

DeKok walked on, his hand behind his back, staring at the ground.

"She *could* have found a temporary shelter for the child. But the important question remains: where can she be?"

Vledder waved his arms around.

"Just about anywhere ... she certainly has the means. According to Henri, Verbruggen arranged a substantial Swiss bank account for her. She can freely access that, after his death. Henri figured that there was more than enough to keep her in wealth for the rest of her life."

DeKok whistled softly.

"It could be a motive."

"I thought about that," laughed Vledder, "but she has an unshakable alibi. The staff of the hospital all agreed that Stella did not leave her bed from Sunday night until at least twenty-four hours after that."

"All right," said DeKok, "it was just a thought."

"But there is something else," said Vledder. "Stella and Henri have no joint property. There was a prenuptial agreement and Henri doesn't get a dime of Verbruggen's money."

"He told you that?"

"No, I found that out myself."

"Dick," teased DeKok, "only a little longer and I can retire completely."

"Yeah, sure," sneered Vledder, "I have heard that for years."

* * *

Lowee, because of his small stature, usually referred to as Little Lowee, rubbed his small hands on his vest and a happy grin lit up his narrow, ferret-like face.

"Lookie, lookie," he chirped gaily, "Da Great Cop hadda

73

minute. Well come, well come!" He cocked his head. "You're sure you gotta time? Or didja have to ask permission from da Commis first?"

DeKok laughed heartily.

"Lowee," he said, "there isn't a Commissaris made who can prevent me from visiting your esteemed establishment."

Followed by Vledder, he waddled to the end of the bar and hoisted himself on his favorite barstool, his back leaning comfortably against the wall. Here he could also keep an eye on the rest of the interior of the old, cozy bar.

Vledder seated himself next to his partner. He was getting used to the dark, intimate bar where the prostitutes gathered between clients and tried to forget the more sordid aspects of the world's oldest profession. Lowee himself was known to be a small-time fence, but had only been caught once, by DeKok. These days he was either more circumspect, or DeKok paid less attention to his nefarious activities. Over the years a real friendship had developed between the small, mousy barkeeper and the rugged old cop. DeKok was the only person in Amsterdam Lowee confided in and with his intimate knowledge of the underworld was always a reliable source of information.

Lowee produced a venerable bottle of cognac, a bottle he kept especially for DeKok. He showed the label and beamed at the appreciative grunts from the gray sleuth.

"Same recipe?" he asked.

DeKok nodded, but did not speak. The question was merely an introduction to a by now almost hallowed tradition. With pleasure he looked on as Lowee produced three large snifters and started to pour.

Vledder raised his glass and sniffed appreciatively. Under DeKok's guidance he was rapidly becoming a connoisseur of good cognac. DeKok held his glass up against the light and waited until Lowee, too, had picked up his glass. With silent enjoyment they took the first sip. DeKok closed his eyes and followed the golden liquid as it found its way to his stomach. Then he opened his eyes and looked at Lowee.

"Do you have any more of these bottles?"

"Yep," answered Lowee proudly, "almost a full case. Gotta real deal on 'em, but I doesn't sell it to nobody else. They got no *taste*."

DeKok took another sip and again enjoyed silently as the precious drink found its way into his innards.

"Lowee," he said after a long pause. "There are times that I positively love life."

"I just knowed you'd like it," grinned Lowee.

Lowee spoke a type of Dutch that even native Dutchmen found hard to understand. His language was the language of the underworld and the gutter. A mixture of several languages with meanings far removed from their original intent and almost all mispronounced. The closest thing to *bargoens*, as it is called, would probably be a mixture of Cockney, Yiddish, Dutch and Papiamento , which is itself a mixture of Dutch, Portuguese and several African dialects.

DeKok was the only cop in the Netherlands who both understood and spoke *bargoens*, but he firmly refused to speak it.

"So, whatsa going atta station, already?" asked Lowee.

DeKok shrugged.

"Busy, as always."

"Got somethin' special like?"

DeKok looked thoughtfully at the bartender

"A few days ago they killed a banker in North."

Lowee bobbed his head.

"I done read about that." He scratched the back of his neck. "I knowed that guy. He done been here coupla times."

"Here?" asked Vledder, surprised.

Lowee did not even look at the younger man. DeKok was a friend, but Vledder was a cop. The fact that DeKok was a friend of Vledder, or the other way around, did not bother Lowee. The foibles of one's friends were overlooked. But that did not mean that Lowee was ready to accept Vledder in his circle of intimates.

"Here?" asked DeKok in turn.

"Yep," said Lowee. "He usta visit Hennie lotsa times in them days. She woulda get him over here for a brew ... you knows, *after*."

"Blonde Hennie?"

"Yep, thatsa one. Atta time she was close, you knows." He pointed over his shoulder. "Rear Fort, just a coupla doors down."

"And Verbruggen was her customer?"

"Sneaky sonofa ..." Lowee broke off, well aware of De-Kok's aversion to strong language. "I means sneaky bast ... well, anyways notta nice guy, you knows."

"How do you mean"

"Well, he tole Hennie all them lies, you knows. Tole her he was just a poor clerk inna bank and datta ... his wife were sick and datte needs to *spare* 'er, you knows. And he done had two kids he hadda put in school. So he wants some credit, you knows, a little time and he couldna pay too much, neither. You got it?"

"And?"

"Hennie believes 'im, you knows, so she done give 'im cut rates. Anyways ... one day she sees da mug inna paper and then it come out he's some kinda big muckedy muck inna bank."

DeKok smiled.

"Hennie upset," he commented.

"You got it. When he comes next time, she lay low, you knows, don't let on she knows. And when he gotta pay, she beat him up widda newspaper and took all 'is loot from da wallet."

DeKok drained his glass.

"And where is Hennie now?"

"She don't *tipple** no more her own self. Saved her dough and buys her own little set-up."

"Where?"

"Old Friend Alley. She gotta coupla broads."

"Madam?"

Lowee had an admiring look on his face.

"Watta business. The gals only get a small part of da loot. Hennie invest da rest for 'em, you knows. Now they can stop workin' when they wants. Sorta retirement, you knows."

DeKok smiled.

"Well, at least she learned something from that banker."

"You gotta do somethin' with da killing?" There was hint of disbelief. "North ain't part of your bailiwick, now, is it?"

"Special instructions from the Judge-Advocate."

"Gettin' anywheres?"

DeKok grimaced.

"I've never seen a murderer with a big `M' on his forehead."

The bartender looked at the clock over the bar.

"Hennie stops by regular about this time. You wanna talk to 'er? You never knows. You got no idea wadda Johns tell them broads."

"I don't think Verbruggen was the type, but I'd like to talk to her."

Lowee motioned to a table near the window and caught the attention of an old, heavily made-up woman.

"Go get Hennie for Mr. DeKok," he called, "then the next one is onna house."

The woman drained her glass and came slowly to her feet.

---

* *tipple* (bargoens) for walking the streets as a prostitute, also *pezen*.

She was back in a short time and raised a thumb to Lowee. Lowee hastened over with a fresh bottle and she regained her seat.

When Lowee had again returned to his place behind the bar, DeKok leaned forward.

"Seen Jimmy Munk, lately?"

"Nah," said Lowee, shaking his head. "He's got some rich dame onna line, these days. She takes care of some rich geezers … she's good at it."

DeKok rubbed the back of his neck.

"Didn't he used to write letters to customers of his girl-friends?

Lowee laughed.

"Blackmail, you means." His hand went to the bottle of cognac, but let go when he saw DeKok shake his head. "Sure," he continued, "still do, as far as I knows. Jimmy Munk don't know better."

A woman entered the bar. Her blonde hair was piled high on her head. She wore a purple sweater and gold-lame slacks with extremely high heels. DeKok recognized her at once. With small steps she came to the bar and shook hands with the old detective. Vledder moved over one stool and she settled herself between the two cops.

DeKok gestured toward the bottle and Lowee produced a fourth glass.

"No, just give me a beer," said Hennie.

Lowee replaced the glass and tapped a beer. He placed the beer in front of Hennie and then carefully pored cognac in the empty snifters.

"You wanted to see me?" asked Blonde Hennie.

DeKok looked at her with admiration.

"You're looking good, Hennie."

"Good feed and a warm stable," she smiled.

"Lowee told me about the banker, Verbruggen, who was one of your customers."

"Oh, yes, the one that got shot this week ... nice crook. Told me had no money, just needed to spare his sickly wife the rigors of sexual intercourse, all that kind of stuff. And I believed him, more fool I."

"Yes," laughed DeKok, "Lowee told me." He paused. "How long was he your customer?" he asked, raising the refilled glass to his nose and inhaling deeply.

"Let me see, now. It must have been about two, or three years. He always came on Fridays, around four in the afternoon." She grinned. "Get it? Came, ha ha."

"Very droll," said DeKok, who had heard every sexual joke and innuendo there was. "Did he ever talk about himself."

Hennie shook her head.

"Yes, sure. But lies, nothing but lies. Once I discovered who he really was, it was over." She took a sip from her beer and then looked at DeKok. "But you know," she continued, "I'm not at all surprised that somebody finally killed him."

"How's that?"

"One time a man came to visit me, an older man, on or about sixty years old. Verbruggen had just left and was still in front of the door. The man pointed and asked if he, Verbruggen I mean, paid well. I looked at him and told him it was none of his business."

"What happened next?"

"He said something like that it was time that someone helped him into a better world, that someone should stop him permanently. He looked at me for a while and then asked me if I knew who that someone might be. He then pointed at himself and said: 'That someone is me.' Then he left. I think he did not want to be where Verbruggen had been, you see."

"What did you do?"

"Nothing. I thought it was just some nut. But when I read in the paper about Verbruggen, I had to think again about that man. And you know what I suddenly realized?"

"What?"

"He meant it."

7

DeKok leaned back in his desk chair.

"Was there a lot of interest?"

Vledder nodded slowly.

"I think the complete cream of Dutch management was at the funeral. I saw Ex-Cabinet Members, former State Secretaries and expensive captains of industry. The top players in most multi-national organizations were present."

A broad grin lit up DeKok's face.

"Well, in view of that much interest, Verbruggen must have been very popular in those circles."

"How do you mean?"

DeKok waved the question away.

"Did Bram Weelen get his pictures?"

"Sure." Vledder laughed at the memory. "Bram knew almost everybody there. He said he had never seen such a gathering of ir-regulars. He even claimed he saw someone who had been in front of his camera for the usual police picture after an arrest."

"Who?"

"Jimmy Munk."

DeKok narrowed his eyes.

"Among *that* gathering?"

"Yes," answered Vledder, "and what's more, he looked like

he belonged."

"What about Carla Heeten?"

"I did not see her."

"Stella LaCroix?"

"Come on DeKok, if I had seen her I would have told you right away, might even have arrested her. I looked especially for her. I was sure she would be attending the funeral of her father." He shook his head sadly. "But she wasn't there."

DeKok rubbed his chin.

"That is indeed remarkable," he commented. "Stella took her father's side after the divorce and I was under the impression there was a strong bond between those two."

"But she wasn't there, all the same."

"Henri?"

Vledder grinned.

"Oh, yes, *he* was there. Very self-effacing, very much in the background, but in such a way that everybody knew he was there."

He consulted his notes.

"He did give an eulogy in the Chapel. Very much prepared and rehearsed. He spoke about the exceptional qualities of the dear departed ... his value to the Bank and he closed his speech with ... the sincere wish that the Amsterdam Police would soon arrest the perpetrator."

"Applause."

Vledder looked surprised.

"In the Chapel? Oh, I see what you mean ... for us. But in that case it is definitely not deserved. I have the feeling that we have never before been so far from a solution." He looked at his partner. "Do you see any light?"

DeKok did not answer. As long as he had no "tired" feet, as long as the legion of tiny devils did not attack his calves with their venomous little pitchforks, he remained hopeful. His "tired" feet had always been a reliable barometer to measure the distance from a solution. So far, he had felt fine and he hoped it would continue.

"Did you see Ms. Kolfs, his ex-wife?"

"No, because of Stella, I took a good look at all women present and she wasn't there. But her son was."

"Marius?"

Vledder snorted.

"He seemed bent on provoking an incident. Everybody was dressed in suits, or dark clothes, but he showed up in the same blue jogging suit we saw at his house. There were not a few critical remarks and somebody wanted to remove him from the Chapel. There was a bit of a scuffle when Marius resisted that attempt." Vledder consulted his notes. "He was clearly upset and yelled:

You have made it into a den of thieves."

"New Testament, I think," said DeKok. "What happened next?"

"The undertaker intervened before it could become a complete riot. He calmed the boy down and made sure he could enter the Chapel. A bit later he was in the front rank around the grave."

"The cleaning of the Temple," said DeKok.

"What!?"

"New Testament, it is in three of the four Gospels. Those were the words Jesus said when He threw the money changers and lenders out of the Temple, He said: *You have made it into a den of thieves.*"

Vledder grinned.

"Why would he think of that text?"

"He is a *Worthy Follower of Christ*, it's a sect," said DeKok. "That's what has kept me busy almost all morning. You see, the behavior of Marius really intrigued me when we visited his mother. I wondered what kind of man he was ... what he did. Why had he stood by his mother after the divorce and why did Stella turn against her mother? Marius, I discovered, has for years been a member of a very strict religious sect ... a sect that does little more than study the Bible. One day, they hope, they will cleanse the earth of all evil."

"He'd be better off getting a job with the police," sneered Vledder. "About as much chance of cleansing the earth, but at least he'll be able to do spot cleaning."

DeKok did not respond to the remark.

"That boy is full of hate against his father. His mother did not want any alimony and Marius has renounced all claims on an eventual inheritance from his father. That has been filed with the Courts."

Vledder looked pensive.

"When did he do that" he asked.

"About four months ago."

"So, Stella inherits everything?"

"Yes."

Vledder made some more entries on his computer.

"Well, it's a motive," he said after a while. "But she has a perfect alibi and ..." He did not finish the sentence. "So Marius has nothing to gain by his father's death," he concluded.

"Not in that way," answered DeKok. "but that does not exclude him as a suspect. Just because he does not gain financially, does not mean he could not have been the killer. A long, burning hatred can also be a motive."

"You think Marius killed his father?"

Again DeKok did not respond. He looked through the drawers of his desk and found a roll of peppermints. Thoughtfully he peeled one off and put it in his mouth. He placed the remains of the roll in his breast pocket.

"That near riot," he said finally, "this morning in the Chapel, somehow doesn't surprise me. According to some of my sources, Marius had also planned to create a disturbance at the baptism in Wester Church, last Sunday. He revealed the plan during a meeting of his sect. One of the other members observed that the baby was blameless and that only God had the right *to visit the sins of the fathers on the children.* Because of that, Marius abandoned his plans."

"A strange guy."

DeKok grunted.

"Yes, a strange person and ... somebody who is very familiar with the Bible."

"Of course," said Vledder, "the text we found in the apartment: *I have called thee by thy name; thou art Mine.*"

8

As DeKok entered the large, busy detective room, one of the Inspectors motioned for him to come over.

"DeKok," he called, "come over here a moment, will you?"

DeKok stepped closer.

"What is it?" he asked.

"You want to handle this?" asked his colleague.

DeKok looked at the group in front of the other's desk. A small, sad, little man in a suit that was too large for him. Two uniformed constables stood on either side. The little man was not hand-cuffed and the constables apparently did not feel it necessary to constrain him in any way. They just stood there, bored, almost disinterested.

"What's the matter with him?" asked DeKok.

One of the constables answered.

"He attacked a woman, a stranger, on the Darmrak."

"Oh?"

"Yes, he jumped in her direction and made stabbing motions," clarified the constable.

"Why?" asked DeKok.

The constable shrugged.

"Because."

"All right, put him in a room."

One of the constables led the man to an interrogation room and the other constable handed a knife to DeKok.

DeKok looked at it. It was a strange type of knife. It had started life as a dinner knife and an untrained hand had used an inadequate stone to file a point on it. With a lot of imagination one could conclude that it resembled a dagger. It was obviously an amateur attempt.

DeKok talked for a few minutes with his colleague at the desk. Vledder walked by and stopped, interested. DeKok waved for him to go to his own desk.

"I'll be right with you," said the gray sleuth.

DeKok went into the interrogation room. The constable helped the man out of his sodden overcoat and provided a towel. After the man had dried himself more or less, the constable held a chair for him and then, with a nod at DeKok, left the room.

DeKok sat down across from the man. He placed the knife on the table between them.

"Is this yours?" he asked.

The little man glanced at the knife, almost shyly.

"Yes," he admitted.

"You threatened a woman with this?"

"I wanted to stab her."

"But why?"

"She reminded me of my own wife."

"You're married?"

"No longer. I'm divorced. She has the children ... all three."

He fumbled in a pocket and produced a wrinkled cigarette. DeKok leaned over and gave him a light.

"I own a small factory. On the Canal. Packing material. It went not bad ... I worked night and day. For her, you see?"

DeKok nodded and gestured to the floor as the man help-lessly looked for an ashtray.

"And for the children," continued the man. "But because I worked so hard, I had little time for my family. You know how it goes ... you want to succeed and you forget what is really important. I bought a house for her."

He lowered his head. Gently DeKok relieved him of the cigarette and crushed it out on the floor.

"One day," said the man, a sob in his voice, "she told me there was another and she wanted a divorce. I was devastated. I didn't want to believe her. But one day she introduced him, the other guy, to me."

He looked at DeKok.

"I told her that if she really felt that this guy could make her happy, she should do it. Divorce me, I mean." He shuddered. "But you don't really know what you're saying at a moment like that. At once I had lost everything: my wife, my children, my house. I could not get over it. I roamed around, neglected my business ... started to drink and within a year I had lost the factory ... bankrupt."

"And all because of your wife?"

He nodded slowly.

"When you start thinking about it, you rebel ... you want vengeance."

DeKok nodded his understanding.

"But why did you attack this strange woman. She wasn't your wife, was she?"

The little man looked surprised.

"Naturally," he said with dignity, "you can't do something like that to the mother of your children."

DeKok leaned back, completely taken aback.

"I see," he said, finally.

He stood up and left the room. He approached the detective who had called him over.

"Get him something warm to drink," advised DeKok. "Then call Social Services. If I were you I would contact the woman he attacked and ask her if she will drop the charges."

"Really?" asked his colleague.

"Yes," said DeKok. "I don't think it will happen again. It was a mistake."

* * *

Vledder held the bullet between thumb and forefinger.

"Pretty heavy caliber ... nine millimeter ... practically undamaged."

"Well, that's just fine for the lab," smiled DeKok. "But we still have to find the weapon."

Vledder rolled the bullet back and forth in his hand.

"It must have lodged in the thick carpet after it exited the body." The young Inspector placed the projectile on his desk and placed a folder on DeKok's desk. "The diagram of where the bullet was found and the report from the Technical Squad."

"Just one bullet?"

Vledder nodded.

"That's all they found and they used a metal detector."

"Are you sure they covered the ground?"

"Sure as I can be," admitted Vledder. "They even searched the ceiling. They checked every room in the place, not just the room where the body was found."

DeKok opened the folder and stared at the diagram.

"At first glance there seem to be few surprises," he said. "Diagonally into the floor ... about a meter from where Verbruggen was found ... lodged in the floor, entry hidden by the carpet. Just about the only thing that's not certain is the position of the shooter."

Vledder came closer and also looked at the diagram.

"Yes, well, I have stared at it for a long time myself and I can't figure it out, either."

DeKok rummaged in a drawer and produced a piece of paper. It was a rough sketch he had made himself at the scene of the crime.

"Because of the immediate effect of the bullet, we can definitely decide on Verbruggen's position."

"How do you mean?"

"Well, he died instantly. Therefore he was not killed anywhere else and then moved. He must have fallen where he was shot. If we accept that and then enter the final resting place of the bullet ... I get a funny feeling."

"I see what you mean. It would have been more logical if the bullet had been found in the wall, or further away from the body."

"Exactly," agreed DeKok. "And that's why there's something fishy about all this," he added.

Vledder sat down on the corner of DeKok's desk.

"If," he said, "we place Verbruggen in a standing position... then it follows that the shooter must have been standing on a chair, or something, in order to get the result we found."

DeKok gave Vledder a serious look.

"It's something entirely different," he said softly.

"What then?" demanded Vledder, irritation on his tone.

DeKok pushed the diagram away.

"Verbruggen wasn't standing," he said. "He also wasn't looking up, as Dr. Koning suggested. It's much more sinister than that ... he was already on his knees."

* * *

Commissaris Buitendam stretched himself and placed folded

hands in front of him on the desk. His aristocratic face was serious.

"This time I will not invite you to sit down, DeKok," he said in his affectated voice. "Just do as you like." He coughed several times for effect. "As you might have guessed, I have discussed with Mr. Schaap your ... eh, precipitous remark that he, Mr. Schaap, is responsible for the death of Mr. Verbruggen." He remained silent for several seconds as if to let that sink in. "Mr. Schaap wishes to speak to you," he added.

"Where?"

"In the Palace of Justice."

"When?"

"At two o'clock."

The gray sleuth looked at his chief suspiciously.

"For a reprimand?"

The Commissaris pressed his hands tighter together. His knuckles turned white and a red blush appeared on his cheeks.

"Mr. Schaap will most certainly convey his displeasure," he said angrily, "and you will admit that your behavior most certainly calls for that."

DeKok shook his head, a determined look on his face.

"In that case I'm not going."

The Commissaris flew out of his chair.

"You are going!" he yelled.

DeKok shook his head again. He spread his feet further apart. There was an immovable quality in his stance.

"I will certainly want to discuss Verbruggen's death with the Judge-Advocate," DeKok said calmly. "But *not*, if I'm judged to be wrong from the outset. And I most certainly am *not* in the mood to be reprimanded by someone as unqualified as Mr. Schaap."

The Commissaris turned red to the roots of his neck.

"Not in the mood!" he roared. "Not in the mood!? Of course you are in the mood. When the Judge-Advocate calls you only have to obey!"

DeKok grinned, disbelief on his face.

"An order?"

Buitendam waved his arms about.

"Exactly, yes ... an order, a direct order from your superior officer. And I can assure you ... if you are not there at two o'clock, I will recommend your immediate dismissal from the force."

DeKok was unmoved.

"Dumb," he said.

Seething with anger, Commissaris Buitendam came from behind his desk and stamping his feet, he pointed at the door.

"OUT!"

* * *

DeKok slipped down in the seat and thought over the latest conversation with the Commissaris. He was not worried about the threat of dismissal. His seniority and reputation was such that he could only be removed from his post in a few ways. He could either voluntarily retire, or he had to be convicted of criminal activity. Or I could die, he thought. But none of these options were likely in the near future. Even insubordination could not remove him. He knew as well as anyone else on the force, that he was the best detective on active duty. His success rate was at least twice that of the next in line. The only thing the powers that be could do was to hold up his promotion. But if it were to be offered, he would certainly refuse it. Primarily because a promotion would also inevitably mean a desk job, which he detested. He was happy were he was ... on the street, mingling with people and, where possible, dispensing his own special brand of justice.

"I despise orders," he growled after a long silence. "Orders are stupid. One should be able to reason with a person, convince him, or her, to do something, or not to do something. Orders merely mean that the person issuing the orders is incapable of reasoning."

Vledder, next to him at the wheel of the old VW, laughed out loud.

"Would it be possible?"

"What?"

"To convince you of anything."

DeKok had to smile. He knew his own faults better than most.

The Palace of Justice appeared in the windshield. When they came closer, they saw broken windows and the walls were covered with graffiti. DeKok snorted.

"If we have sunk so low that we deface the symbols of justice ..." He did not finish the sentence, but pointed at a parking spot on the other side of the canal.

Vledder reacted immediately by crossing the bridge and parking in what must have been the only free spot for several blocks.

They left the car and walked back to the bridge and from there to the side door of the Palace of Justice.

As DeKok pushed against the heavy door, it was suddenly opened wider, a man slipped by them and disappeared with quick steps in the direction of the inner city.

DeKok stared after the disappearing man. He had recognized him. He turned to Vledder.

"You know who that was?"

"No," said Vledder, "but this morning I saw him in the chapel at Verbruggen's funeral. And that wasn't the first time I've seen him. He was also at the baptism."

"Right," said DeKok, "that was Jean-Paul Dervoor ... Managing Director of Electronics International."

Vledder looked back, but the man had disappeared. He turned back toward DeKok.

"The man ... the man who introduced Verbruggen to Carla Heeten."

* * *

Lieutenant Wamel* of the State Police greeted DeKok heartily. They had known each other off and on since the time they were both constables. Now the Lieutenant was in charge of the detachment that protected the Palace of Justice. His troops also provided protection for the various Judges-Advocate and Justices who worked in the building. In addition to the lower courts and Magistrate's Courts, the building also housed a District Court and a Court of Appeals. The Supreme Court of the Netherlands has its own building in The Hague, not too far from the Peace Palace, which houses the International Court of Justice.

"What are you doing here?" asked Wamel.

"I have been commanded into the presence of Mr. Schaap," said DeKok.

Wamel grimaced.

"I don't know what's the matter with that man, lately. He's completely out of his normal routine and is as nervous as a cat. This week he even managed to appear in court without any of the necessary paperwork."

"Outside his nerves," grinned Vledder.

DeKok ignored the remark and leaned closer to Wamel.

"Did Dervoor of Electronics International come to see him

---

* The Dutch State Police uses Army ranks.

as well? I just saw him leave."

"Quite a while," responded Wamel. "He was there for more than an hour and during all that time there were strict orders not to interrupt, for whatever reason." He looked at a schedule. "But he's available now. Shall I announce you?"

"Not me," said Vledder. "I want no part of it. If DeKok gets going, Mr. Schaap may be going to the hospital with a heart attack."

* * *

The office of Mr. Schaap was an impersonal room, relatively small. His desk was the standard institutional desk. For a Judge-Advocate, the office was almost shabby.

Mr. Schaap stood up when DeKok entered and reached out a hand across the desk. Solemnly the two men shook hands.

"Please sit down, Inspector," said Schaap in a cool, impersonal voice. "I understand that there are a few misunderstandings between us that need to be dealt with." He waited for DeKok to seat himself. "Commissaris Buitendam has informed me that you blame me personally for certain events. You must realize that I would never have credited such stories, if it weren't for the fact that you have an excellent reputation as a police officer as well as a detective."

DeKok smiled politely. He was determined to control himself at all costs. There was no profit, he realized, in exacerbating the differences between them. It would harm his case, his investigation.

"You flatter me," said DeKok.

"Not at all. When I heard that my banker friend Verbruggen —we both studied for the Law—was being threatened with certain letters, I immediately thought of you. You may certainly consider that a compliment." Schaap paused. "Therefore," he continued, "your ... eh, accusation that I could have led him to his death was ... without merit."

"He contacted you before he made the appointment?"

"Yes," nodded Schaap, "he called me at home on Sunday. He had just found a letter among Saturday's mail wherein he was invited to come to an apartment in Mill's Quarter."

"And then?"

"I told him to go. I advised him to listen to what they had to say ... find out the conditions. It never occurred to me that Albert would be killed."

"Why did you not inform me?"

The Judge-Advocate spread both hands in a gesture of surrender.

"I did not think it necessary at that time," he said. There was a hint of apology in his tone. "Perhaps after Albert had heard the conditions, the demands, perhaps even some clues, we would have had a basis to determine our position. At that time I would most certainly have consulted you." He scratched his forehead. "But I must emphasize that I was surprised by the death of my friend ... and deeply shocked."

"And the disappearance of Stella and her baby?"

Schaap shrugged.

"That puzzles me too. Perhaps Stella has, despite our precautions, learned something about those threatening letters and she wants to make sure her child is safe."

DeKok nodded agreeably.

"That sounds reasonable. But I cannot help but be surprised that she hasn't tried to contact you in any way. Did you speak to Henri LaCroix at all?"

"Certainly. He calls me daily. It is a difficult time for Henri. Not just the disappearance of his wife, but Albert's death has considerable ramifications for the Ysselstein Bank."

"Such as?"

"Apparently Verbruggen has made contracts, promised investments ... but there are no clear records."

Mr. Schaap seemed suddenly stunned as DeKok's eyebrows performed some impossible gymnastics. If Vledder had been present he would have enjoyed watching the Judge-Advocate's reaction. DeKok was oblivious to the effect. The display was over before it was clearly registered and Mr. Schaap blinked his eyes several times, hardly believing what he had seen.

"A motive for murder?" suggested DeKok.

"Eh, what?" asked Schaap, still confused.

"The incomplete, or missing records ... a motive for murder?"

"Perhaps. It is one of the reasons why I am in almost constant contact with Henri LaCroix. The central question remains, of course, who would benefit from Albert's death." DeKok opened his mouth, but Schaap waved a hand. "I have already ordered a complete audit of the bank." He let out a short, barking laugh. "Believe me, Inspector, I keep myself informed."

"Have you ever heard of Jimmy Munk?"

Schaap looked pensively into the distance.

"I believe he is a crook."

DeKok nodded.

"He writes blackmail letters."

"I think I may have prosecuted him at one time." The Judge-Advocate fell silent. The subject did not seem to interest him very much.

DeKok rubbed the bridge of his nose with a little finger and remained silent as well. Finally he stopped rubbing and looked at his finger in wonderment.

"You know Carla Heeten?" he asked suddenly.

Schaap seemed to jump in his chair.

"You ... eh, you mean the ... young lady who lives in the apartment in which Albert was found?"

"That's the one."

The jurist coughed.

"I knew that Albert entertained certain ... eh, relations with the young lady."

"So you don't know her personally?"

Schaap started to adjust his necktie which was knotted to perfection. He looked at DeKok and then averted his eyes.

"I ... I visited her once or twice."

"Do you have a key to her apartment?"

Mr. Schaap seemed to have regained his courage. He stood up. There was anger in his voice when he spoke.

"I am not responsible for my private life to *you!*" The last word was shouted out loud. He came from behind his desk. "As usual, I will keep track of your progress through the reports you will send me," said Schaap, formally.

DeKok stood up. He understood that Mr. Schaap considered the interview concluded. He walked toward the door, but with the doorknob already in his hand, he turned once more.

"Tell me, Mr. Schaap, what did Jean-Paul Dervoor say to you?"

9

The two Inspectors waved goodbye to Lieutenant Wamel as they left the old, run-down and defaced Palace of Justice. Vledder laughed about what DeKok told him.

"How did he react?"

"He looked as if he saw water burning," grinned DeKok. "He clearly did not expect the question. I've seldom seen anyone look so stupid."

"Did he say anything about it?"

"I didn't want to press him, so I just left it there. I said good-bye and left. I don't need the same situation as with Buitendam."

"Out?"

"Exactly."

In silence they walked across the bridge to where the old VW was parked. Vledder unlocked the car and looked pensively over the roof of the car at his partner.

"But still," he began, "your question wasn't all that crazy. It would be nice to know what Schaap and Dervoor discussed. Does he know anything about the murder? It is certainly possible. After all, we can safely assume that Jean-Paul Dervoor, too, has a key to the apartment. For that alone, he's a possible suspect."

DeKok nodded slowly, leaning his arms on the car.

"I've been thinking about the key situation. I actually

thought about asking Carla Heeten for a list of all the key holders." He grinned without mirth. "I decided against it."

They opened the doors and stepped into the car. Vledder started the engine and after only the third try, it caught. Rattling and shaking he pulled out of the parking spot, fiddling with the manual choke.

"Why?" asked Vledder when they had reached an area with less traffic.

"What do you mean?" asked DeKok.

"Why did you decide against it?"

"Oh, that. Well, in the first place I don't think that Carla will give me a complete list ... especially not if she has been able to discuss it with her clients. Besides, apparently it's custom to lend the key to whoever. Some may have had duplicates made, without telling Carla ... the number of possibilities becomes endless" He shook his head sadly. "And it's also possible that Verbruggen opened the door with his own key and then later opened the door for his killer, a person without a key. No, the key situation isn't going to help us at the moment. It was practically a constant 'open house' at that apartment." He glanced at Vledder. "If you ask me, I think that even our respectable Judge-Advocate has a key."

"Schaap ... really?"

Vledder stopped for a red light.

"Why do you think so?"

"I asked him."

Vledder shook his head.

"Isn't that going a bit far? I mean, to ask the Judge-Advocate if he visits the ladies?"

The light went to green and Vledder pulled up in second gear. Groaning and moaning the vehicle moved.

"Are you deliberately trying to break it?" asked DeKok. "If you are, stop it. We're not going to get a new vehicle until every other cop in the Netherlands has been supplied first. It's one of the little tricks the higher-ups play with me, because I won't dance to their tune."

Vledder growled, but took pity on the aging vehicle.

"Besides," continued DeKok, dismissing the subject car, "it's not so far-fetched. Carla told us that she had an extensive and influential clientele. When I remarked on her beauty louder than I intended, she said she would complain about me to a Judge. She swallowed the second word, but I'm sure it was meant to be 'Advocate' and there is no reason to suspect any other Judge-Advocate but Schaap."

Vledder looked worried.

"A powerful combination," he said. "Verbruggen, Dervoor and Schaap ... banking, industry and justice ... in other words: politics. All three of them have a lot of friends."

They passed the Royal Palace and Vledder devoted himself to the busy traffic on the Dam, Amsterdam's Central Square.

"Well," said Vledder, as they turned into Warmoes Street, "if the motive for the murder is in *those* circles, we can forget about penetrating it."

DeKok was genuinely shocked.

"Forget nothing!" he exclaimed. "If the Judge-Advocate thinks he can flatter me into whitewashing his own dirty laundry, as well as that of his friends, *he* can forget it. No, no, in that case he's bet on the wrong horse, or rather ... he just embraced a Trojan Horse."

"All right," said Vledder, "the ball is in our court, the bases are loaded, let's punt."

He could mix metaphors as easily as anyone.

* * *

Meindert Post the Watch Commander usually spoke several decibels louder than most people. This time he outdid himself.

"DEKOK!"

His voice bounced off the walls and reverberated long after he had closed his mouth again.

DeKok pushed his hat further back on his head and sauntered over to the railing. He and Post had both been born on the former island of Urk, now a hill in the endless flatland of what had been the bottom of the Zuyder Zee. They had gone to school together in the small, one room, village school and DeKok was well acquainted with Meindert's volume. It was always a wonder to DeKok that the man did not rip his vocal cords. The gray sleuth leaned over the railing.

"Did you call me, Meindert," he whispered.

The irony was lost on the Watch Commander.

"There's a guy waiting for you upstairs," he roared.

"What kind of a guy?"

Meindert pulled a face.

"A slippery customer, if you ask me. I'm sure I have seen him in the Quarter at one time or another."

"Jimmy Munk?"

"That's the one. I told him you weren't here, but he wanted to wait for you."

DeKok nodded and together with Vledder he climbed the stairs. Vledder was sure that Munk must have been able to follow the conversation word for word, at least Meindert's part.

"Did you know he'd come here?" asked Vledder.

"No, But I'm not surprised. Blackmailers are always very careful. You want to bet that he's just here to tell us he's innocent."

"We'll see," laughed Vledder.

Upstairs, on the bench outside the detective room was Jimmy Munk, He was expensively dressed and the effect was overwhelming. The coat was too yellow and too expensive. The gold bracelet in addition to the watch on one wrist and the three gold bracelets on the other wrists were too much as well. Heavy rings hid most of his fingers. When he saw the Inspectors, he stood up and came nearer.

"DeKok," he said, "I need to talk to you."

The detective opened the door and gestured for Jimmy to follow.

"How long have you been waiting?"

"About an hour," was the answer.

"In that case," said DeKok, "it must be important. Why don't you sit down."

Jimmy first took off his expensive overcoat and draped it over the back of the chair. With fussy movements he pulled up the legs of his trousers and carefully lowered himself in the chair.

DeKok threw his hat and coat in the direction of the peg. The hat hit, but the coat fell on the floor. Then he sat down behind his desk and leaned both elbows on the desk. He rested his chin in his folded hands. Vledder unobtrusively slipped behind his own desk, next to DeKok's and activated his computer.

DeKok stared openly at his visitor. Under the yellow overcoat he wore a purple jacket, a pink shirt and cream colored slacks. A gold chain held the hand-painted tie in place. Jimmy Munk was over fifty, but he was well preserved. The hair was delicately tinted and his fingernails were polished. He had undergone at least one face lift.

"Get it off your chest," said DeKok pleasantly.

"You know that I have an ongoing affair with Carla Heeten." said Jimmy. He moved in his chair and flicked away an imaginary speck of dust from his trousers. "A nice girl. You met her. Beautiful, too. But sloppy. Careless. She lives as if there's no

tomorrow, know what I mean? Well, a woman like that sometimes gets into trouble."

"And that happened?"

Jimmy Munk did not answer. He placed his hands on his
knees and stared at the wall behind DeKok. He seemed uncertain,
as if he was trying to make up his mind.

"Well," urged DeKok. "What's the matter with Carla?"

"She's got a boy-friend."

"What sort of boy-friend?"

"What the British call a 'toy-boy.' A body builder ... you
know, more brawn than brains. Of course, it's just an infatuation,
but for now she's crazy about that guy."

DeKok looked suspicious.

"Are you trying to tell me that you came here to tell me
about your love life?"

Jimmy Munk shook his head.

"No, I don't need you for that."

"Then get to the point."

"Well, this Robbie ... Beau Robbie they call him."

"Is that his name?"

"That's what he's called. I don't know his real name. I also
don't know where he comes from." He leaned closer to DeKok.
"Well, as I said, this Beau Robbie is getting a bit curious about
Carla's ... eh, clients. You know what she does, don't you?" Without waiting for an answer, he continued. "Well, Robbie is curious
about the visitors to Carla's apartment. You understand? And
Carla has loose lips, you see. Imagine, she's told this guy everything."

"How do you know?"

"She told me herself. She was in trouble and came to see
me."

"What sort of trouble?"

"That dead guy in her apartment, that banker."

"Verbruggen?"

Munk nodded slowly.

"Yes. Carla told me this banker had received threatening letters. They were going to kidnap his grandson. Well, when I heard that, I started to worry, you understand? I mean, I'm not exactly ... I have a record. You may know that and if you don't I'm telling you now. But a murder is a bit much, don't you think? You understand, DeKok? Besides, it's so ... so stupid. You don't kill the goose that lays the golden eggs, now, you just don't. And I never ..."

DeKok held up a hand, stemming the flow of words.

"What *are* you trying to tell me?"

Jimmy Munk swallowed hard. His face was gray.

"That ... that I had nothing to do with that killing ... that murder. I didn't kill that guy." He paused. "And I also didn't write those letters."

DeKok smiled grimly.

"And I'm supposed to believe that?"

"Yes, you must believe that," answered Jimmy softly.

It sounded like a prayer.

DeKok merely stared at the blackmailer. In his heart remained the suspicion.

"And what about this guy ... this Robbie?"

Jimmy Munk bowed his head.

"Carla, Carla thinks *he* did it."

"What!?"

With a strangely distorted face Jimmy looked from Vledder to DeKok and back again. His face-lifted face did not allow the expression he apparently was desperate to convey.

"Beau Robbie ... Robbie was blackmailing him."

* * *

After Jimmy left the detective room with an admonition to hold himself available for the police, Vledder made some final entries on his computer and hit the print button. Several versions of their latest findings in report form started to fill the out-tray. Later they would determine which reports to submit and which to destroy. All the information was available and that was enough for De-Kok. Vledder more and more agreed with him. It was important to decide what to report and to whom.

As the printer started humming, Vledder moved his chair closer to DeKok's desk.

"What do you say about that?" he wondered.

DeKok smiled.

"Nothing. You heard, I was right. Jimmy only came to tell us he's innocent."

"But that story about Robbie?"

"Oh, I'm sure it contains a grain of truth and we will certainly pursue it. Jimmy isn't stupid. If we could easily blow his story apart, he wouldn't have come here. I'm sure that Carla has a boyfriend on the side and I'm also certain that he's called 'Beau Robbie.' I'm also convinced that he's interested in Carla's clients. But that he actually practices blackmail, or even more importantly, killed Verbruggen, is something that's a wide open question."

"But," replied Vledder, "Carla thinks he did it. Surely she has some reason to think so?"

DeKok looked pensive.

"It would," he said, "solve a lot of problems for Jimmy. I'm sure he'd like it to be true."

"How's that?"

"As I said. Blackmailers are careful. If Robbie indeed killed Verbruggen ... then Jimmy is out of the woods. He will no longer be a suspect and he has, at the same time, eliminated a rival in love."

"Some love. But you're right."

DeKok grinned.

"We have to be sure. Also, we have to be very careful with any statements from Carla. I think it's a bit strange that all of a sudden she pours out her heart to Jimmy."

"I don't understand that."

"Beau Robbie," said DeKok, squinting his eyes. "Beau Robbie ... the name is an indication. I'm sure he's a handsome guy. And young, muscular, handsome guys cost money, lots of money. He may be a call-boy, you see. Same profession as Carla, except in this case *she* pays. If Carla wants to get rid of an expensive and perhaps bothersome boyfriend ..." He did not finish the sentence. "People who live in that sort of environment, often have their own codes of conduct."

"But I still want to know who this Beau Robbie really is," said Vledder with determination.

DeKok walked to the peg and took his hat. He bent over and picked up his coat.

"I want to know that as well," he said. "And do you know who can help us with that?"

"Little Lowee," laughed Vledder.

"Exactly."

They walked toward the door when the phone on Vledder's desk rang suddenly. Vledder walked back to pick it up. He listened for a few minutes. DeKok walked back to the desk.

"Something up?"

Vledder covered the mouthpiece.

"They just found Jean-Paul Dervoor."

"Dead?"

"Yes."

"Where?"

"You guessed it. In Carla Heeten's apartment."

10

There was a long, rectangular living room with modern furniture. Almost in the center, within the circle of light thrown by a pink, standing lamp, on a white carpet was the body of a man.

DeKok looked around. He had seen the decor before.

Jean-Paul Dervoor, once the Managing Director of Electronics International was on his left side, leaning on a bent elbow. Both knees had been pulled up, as if in the foetal position.

DeKok knelt down and looked into a set of dead, brown eyes. The mouth was partially open and a narrow trail of blood showed from one corner of the mouth across the cheek. Under the chin, just below the Adam's apple and just above the collar he discovered a round hole ... an almost perfectly round hole, a little over a centimeter wide. Blood had stained the beige sweater.

DeKok looked again at the eyes. Was it there, or did he imagine a look of fear in the strangely silent eyes?

Vledder knelt down next to his partner.

"Shot?"

"Yes," answered DeKok, "and in exactly the same manner as the previous killing. It looks like some sort of ritual."

"Or execution," opined Vledder, "I mean ... the shot in the neck."

DeKok did not answer, but looked closer at the knees of the

brown slacks. Small particles from the carpet were clearly visible. He took one more look at the dead eyes and raised himself to his feet. There was a worried look on his face.

He admitted to himself that Dervoor's death had surprised him. It did not fit in the theory he was building up in his mind. The murder of Verbruggen had suddenly gained an extra dimension.

He looked at the position of the corpse and could still see some faint outlines on the carpet where the position of the previous corpse had been marked. Who was the man, or woman, cold-blooded enough to kill two people in the same way, on the same spot? An idiot? A maniac? What sort of cynicism drove him, or her? He nodded to himself. That was it ... cynicism. The murders contained a chilling, cynical character.

He turned and stared for several seconds at the statuette of the Pierrot on the whatnot. He forced himself to ignore it. Because he knew he would find a piece of paper there, a piece of paper with a by now familiar text.

Detective-Inspector Ping entered the room. For a relatively small man, he had a heavy step.

"For the time being I parked the guy at the station house," he said. "That's Wadden Street station," he added.

"What guy?"

Ping gestured toward the body on the floor.

"The one who discovered him here. That way you can take your time talking to him, later. He's not going anywhere and here he would just be in the way."

"A guy with a key?" asked DeKok.

"Yes," laughed Ping. "He had a key for the apartment. Couple of years. Apparently he came every Wednesday to get laid."

DeKok shook his head disapprovingly.

"That's called an *erotic intermezzo*. It sounds better."

Ping was not interested.

"When I heard that another body was found in this apartment, I called you guys immediately. I figured they were connected."

"In what way?"

Ping shrugged his shoulders.

"Those are your worries," answered Ping with a grin of malicious delight. "The Judge-Advocate insisted that you handle the case. So ..." He did not finish his sentence, but pointed at the body. "You know him?"

DeKok nodded vaguely.

"We saw him only this afternoon at the Palace of Justice. He was in a hurry."

"To meet his maker," commented Ping.

Dr. Koning squeezed by two uniformed constables. DeKok walked towards him, and shook his hand.

"Thank you for coming, Doctor," said DeKok meaning it.

"I've been here before, haven't I?" asked Koning. He peered at the corpse.

"You remember that correctly, Doctor," said DeKok. "About ten days ago. But this time it's somebody else."

Dr. Koning pulled up on the striped trousers he always wore and as he knelt down, he flipped aside the slips of his tailcoat. He took off the greenish Garibaldi hat and held it in one hand. The examination did not take long. Assisted by Vledder he came to his feet.

"The man is dead," said the doctor, "and not long."

"Thank you Doctor," said DeKok formally. Then: "How long?"

"An hour, maybe a little longer. There is no indication of rigor mortis."

"What about the pupils?"

"I saw nothing peculiar. The cause of death, like the last time, is a bullet ... an aimed neck shot."

Koning replaced his hat and used a slip from his coat to polish up his pince-nez.

"Am I going to get more like this?" he asked.

"As long as I haven't found the killer," apologized DeKok, "... a repeat is always possible."

Dr. Koning pointed at the door.

"Why don't you seal off the place. That way it cannot happen again."

DeKok smiled.

"The mere fact that a murder victim has been found here twice, does not give us the authority to seal off a private residence forever. Besides," he added, "the killer can operate anywhere."

DeKok turned to Vledder.

"When did you release the apartment?"

Vledder consulted his notebook.

"Last Tuesday. Last Tuesday, after the first murder. As soon as the Technical Squad was finished and the clean-up detail had been through, I called Carla Heeten and told her she could use the apartment again."

"And that happened?"

"I presume so."

DeKok nodded and looked at Ping.

"That guy you have on ice, came every Wednesday?"

"Yes," said Ping, "for several years. He almost had a heart attack when he found the body and fled in a panic."

DeKok pulled out his lower lip and let it plop back.

"Where?" he asked musingly. "Where was Carla?"

Ping and Vledder looked nonplussed.

"What do you mean?" asked Ping.

"Think," said DeKok. "That guy didn't come here to watch

television."

Vledder was the first to react.

"You're right ... she should have been here."

* * *

DeKok strolled down the corridors of the Wadden Street station. Despite his obvious ease, he felt a stranger. DeKok did not like modern buildings. There was too much space, too much light and no atmosphere, no sense of belonging. The walls were bare and painted in an undefinable institutional color. It was almost as sterile as a hospital. No hidden whispers of hope, happiness and pain as in the old station house at Warmoes Street. The building did not feel human enough for DeKok.

A constable walked ahead to point the way. The young woman was the only cheerful note around, thought DeKok. She was small and pert and the uniform made her look trim and capable.

"He's in here, sir," she pointed.

"Thank you," said DeKok as he opened the door.

A man was seated on a chair behind a table. It was the typical interrogation room, albeit cleaner and less personal than the dank cubicles at Warmoes Street. Stop it, DeKok, he admonished himself, next thing you know, you'll be telling yourself you actually *like* slum conditions.

Instead he concentrated on the man. DeKok estimated him to be in his late fifties. He was dressed in an expensive, dark-blue suit, including a waistcoat. Stiff and respectable, like a sexton on Sunday. DeKok reached out a hand.

"My name is DeKok," he introduced himself, "DeKok with kay-oh-kay. I'm an Inspector. I wanted to have a little chat with you about your ... eh, your discovery this afternoon."

115

The man reacted nervously. His face was red. He tapped his watch with a forefinger.

"I've been waiting here for almost forty-five minutes," he protested. "I am not a prisoner. I have not even been arrested."

DeKok gave him a winning smile.

"I interrupted my investigations in the apartment to spare you any further waiting." He took a notebook from his pocket and placed it on the table, while he pulled out a chair for himself.

"What's your name?"

"Charles ... Charles Broos." He pointed at the notebook. "I would prefer it if I were not identified by name. My relationship with Miss Carla is of a ... confidential nature."

"I understand."

"To tell you the truth, I'm sorry I notified the police. Perhaps it would have been better if I had just left."

"So you could be accused of being the murderer?"

Charles Broos looked frightened.

"That is nonsense," he sputtered. "You must know that. The man was dead when I arrived."

"What time was that?"

"Five o'clock. I always come at five o'clock. Every Wednesday. Carla expects me. She waits for me."

DeKok leaned closer.

"How long have you been visiting Carla?"

"Almost three years. I was introduced by a business acquaintance. He invited me over one night and introduced us."

DeKok doodled in his notebook.

"You must practically have met the killer, this afternoon. That's how close you were to the time of death. Did you see anything peculiar ... out of the ordinary? Something that was different from other Wednesdays?"

"No."

116

"But yet," insisted DeKok, "Carla was not there ... was not waiting for you."

Broos swallowed.

"You're right ... Carla wasn't there. Instead there was a corpse."

"Was the front door locked?"

"Yes."

"Did you touch anything ... move the body?"

Charles Broos shook his head vehemently.

"No, I just leaned over him. I saw at once that he was dead."

"And there was nobody else?"

The man shrugged.

"I can't say and I don't know. I saw nobody else. Usually Carla meets me in the foyer. When I did not see her there, I went into the room, but I went no farther."

DeKok placed both hands in the back of his neck and stretched.

"So," he said, suppressing a yawn, "it's possible that somebody was in one of the other rooms ... for instance ... the bedroom."

Broos nodded vaguely.

"Perhaps ... as I said, I did not look anywhere else. As soon as I saw the corpse I had only one thought ... away ... police."

DeKok smiled politely.

"Very understandable." He paused and looked at the man across from the bare table. "Did you know that another man has been murdered in Carla's apartment?"

Charles Broos moved in his chair. He took a handkerchief from his pocket and wiped his forehead.

"I ... eh ... I read about t-that," he stuttered. "Not t-too long ago ... in the p-paper."

"And you visited her last week?"

"Yes."

"Did Carla tell you anything about the murder?"

Broos shook his head.

"I did think she was a bit nervous ... restless."

"Did *you* bring up the murder?"

"No."

DeKok lowered his arms and placed them flat on the table.

"Apart from this business acquaintance who introduced you, do you know any other people who visit Carla?"

Broos looked angry.

"No," he said in a loud voice. "No," he repeated, a bit softer, "and I don't want to know them, either."

With slow movements DeKok put away his notebook. He placed his elbows on the table and rested his chin on his folded hands.

"Have you ever received any threatening letters?"

Large drops of sweat appeared on Broos' forehead while he paled visibly. One drop of sweat found its way to his eyebrows and remained suspended at one corner above the left eye.

DeKok sensed the tension.

"Have you received threatening letters?" repeated DeKok.

With a shaking hand Charles Broos felt for an inside pocket and came back with a brown envelope.

"If ... if I don't pay," he whispered, "I'll be killed ... just like Verbruggen."

11

DeKok tapped a thick finger on the brown envelope on his desk.

"But this one is different," he exclaimed, "It's not at all the same as the ones I got after the baptism ... Verbruggen's letters."

Vledder looked noncommittal.

"It's a death threat, as well as blackmail."

DeKok nodded slowly and dipped a hand in a side pocket. The hand emerged with a piece of licorice between two fingers. DeKok looked at it and dusted it off. Then he put it in his mouth.

"Yes, this letter *does* give the impression that the writer is responsible for Verbruggen's death. Charles Broos believes it. He's scared stiff and ready to pay."

"Fifty thousand guilders?"

DeKok smiled.

"A modest request. I inquired and Charles Broos is worth a lot more than that. He's a Director in a number of concerns and has large sums of money at his disposal."

"Perhaps the blackmailer is less well informed," said Vledder easily.

DeKok did not answer. He picked up the brown envelope and tossed it in his desk drawer with the other letters. Then he slammed shut the drawer with a motion of barely controlled rage.

"Something doesn't fit," he said with conviction. "This letter is different in tone, different in style. It is much more direct and was typed on a different machine ... Besides, this time money is actually demanded."

Vledder manipulated his computer.

"Do we have any old letters from Jimmy Munk?"

"You want to compare them? Can you do that on that thing?"

"Now I can," answered Vledder. "I have a scanner now and the other letters are already in the system. Of course, I need the actual specimen of the previous letters to ..."

DeKok held up a hand.

"Enough! I don't want to know. But if you're looking for old evidence, talk to Dishoven." DeKok referred to the archivist and administrator of the station house. "He's just as much a squirrel as you. But," added DeKok with a certain satisfaction, "he doesn't use an electric wonder box. He files stuff the old fashioned way ... in dusty attics."

Vledder laughed.

"I doubt that," he responded. "But you think it's a good idea? To check the old evidence, I mean?"

"Oh, yes, no doubt about it."

"You see," said Vledder, "I thought it might be just the type of stunt Jimmy Munk would pull. First he tells us that Robbie, his rival for Carla's charms, is the blackmailer and then he collects the money himself."

"I followed that," said DeKok. "No need to belabor the point."

"All right, all right. But something else ... what sort of deal did you make with Charles Broos?"

DeKok rubbed his chin.

"It wasn't easy to convince him to cooperate. He'd much rather pay the money and be done with it. Only after I convinced him that the first fifty thousand was no more than a down payment, that he would have to go on paying ... did he become a little more anxious to help. As soon as he receives further instructions about time and place of payment, he'll call at once."

"That's all?"

"What do you mean?"

Vledder pointed at his computer.

"The marking of the money, the recording of the serial numbers, the setting of a trap."

DeKok smiled.

"We still have to work that out. Charles Broos was still much too preoccupied with his discovery. After all, it's not exactly an everyday occurrence for the average citizen to discover a corpse."

"Did he know Dervoor?"

DeKok shrugged and unwrapped a forgotten toffee he found in the shadow of his unused computer terminal. The keyboard was not hooked up and nobody knew where it was. Not that it mattered, DeKok had never even switched on the machine.

"Broos told me," he said, chewing diligently on the toffee, "that he had been introduced to Carla by a business acquaintance and he did not know any of her other visitors. I did have the feeling that he was lying and that he knew both victims, Verbruggen and Dervoor. Possibly he knew them very well."

"How's that?"

"All these top players in business know each other. Their personal and business concerns are often connected in one way or another. They form some sort of ..."

"Clique," supplied Vledder.

"You're thinking of what Ms. Kolfs told us."

Vledder nodded and hit several keys on his computer.

"She said: *Yes, I knew that whole clique surrounding my*

husband. And later, when you said something about the word being unpleasant, she said: *It's the only word that fits. My husband often flirted with criminal activities and the people he surrounded himself with, were of the same shady type.* "

"You got all that in there?"

Vledder nodded impatiently. There was a painful look on his face. DeKok looked concerned.

"Something the matter?"

"Perhaps," said Vledder, wiping his lips, "perhaps the killer made a mistake."

"Mistake?"

"Yes, perhaps he was waiting for Charles Broos."

"And Dervoor showed up first," commented DeKok, thoughtfully.

"Hey, DeKok!" yelled one of the detectives closest to the door of the room. "Somebody here to see you!"

DeKok waved in acknowledgement and watched the visitor approach. DeKok watched him carefully. About twenty-five, he thought. Well dressed in a tweed suit. With a faint smile the young man approached DeKok.

"You are Inspector DeKok?" he asked.

"At your service," said DeKok as he pointed at a chair for his visitor.

Before sitting down, the young man made a stiff bow.

"I am Jean Baptiste Dervoor ... the eldest son."

DeKok shook hands with his visitor.

"My condolences," DeKok gravely said. "The sudden passing of your father must have been a shock to you and your family."

Young Dervoor nodded and sat down.

"Mother asked me to talk to you. She can't understand it. She wants to know more about that apartment ... the apartment of that young lady where my father was ... a regular visitor. From what we've heard, it's the same apartment where Mr. Verbruggen was found dead."

"Yes," agreed DeKok. "And the same killer." He paused. "The manner in which it happened, the *modus operandi,* is almost identical."

Jean Baptiste swallowed.

"You mean that my father and Mr. Verbruggen were killed by the same man?"

"Exactly. But it is not at all certain that the killer is a man."

"It could have been a woman?"

Vledder, who was prone to state the obvious, shook his head silently. Really, he thought, if not a man it has to be a woman, What other possibilities are there?

DeKok remained polite.

"Indeed," he said in answer to Dervoor's question.

"But what's the sense of it all?" exclaimed young Dervoor. "My father worked hard. He was the head of an enormous concern, gave work to tens of thousand. Why would a man like that be ..."

DeKok interrupted.

"You knew Mr. Verbruggen?"

"Certainly. He was a friend of father's."

"How long?"

"As long as I can remember. As a child I used to go on vacation with the Verbruggen family. Usually to Switzerland, they have a chalet there."

"And you know Stella?"

A small smile spread over Dervoor's face.

"Yes, she was the love of my life ... of course, we were very young. She was my first love, anyway," he grinned. "I liked her very much. I could never resist pulling her pigtails. And we saw a lot of each other as teenagers."

"But it did not result in marriage?"

"No, she married Henri LaCroix ... just a bank clerk."

"Can you shed any light on her disappearance?"

A sober expression came into Jean's eyes.

"I think she's afraid ... she's hiding out somewhere, with her child."

DeKok shrugged. He had figured as much himself.

"She did not attend her father's funeral. I'm a bit curious about that. Apparently she and her father were very close."

Jean Baptiste looked surprised.

"Stella?" he said, shaking his head. "No, you have that wrong. Stella and her father weren't close at all. On the contrary, they often fought tooth and nails. Stella ran away several times."

DeKok glanced at Vledder who was making notes.

"But, she took her father's side when it came to a divorce between her parents."

"Just money," grinned Jean Baptiste. "Verbruggen was a symbol of wealth and power ... things like that just didn't interest her mother and brother."

"And Stella?"

"She pursued both with a passion."

"How?"

Dervoor made a vague gesture.

"I know her very well." It sounded irritated. "I've known her for years. If Stella wanted something ... it just ... happened."

"What about Marius? Did he hate his father?"

Jean Baptiste Dervoor thought for a while.

"Marius is a strange one," he said after a while. "Always has been. It's true, he and his father didn't get along. And Verbruggen was difficult to get along with ... he was demanding, he expected a lot from his children. But I think that his father was too big for

124

him ... too remote ... too distant to really hate." He looked at the Inspector. "Why don't you ask me if I hated my father?"

"Did you?"

"No, I loved my father," said Jean loudly, passionately. "I admired his drive, his spirit, his capacity for work. He was a great man." He moved in his chair and leaned forward. His face was paler, but there was a wild look in his eyes. "And I personally will see to it that his killer is found ... my father shall have justice." He pointed at DeKok. "You're an accomplice in his death."

"Really?" asked DeKok calmly. "I didn't have anything to do with his death."

Jean Baptiste shook his head, as if to clear his mind.

"No, not that way," he exclaimed, "but if you had been quicker ... more capable ... if you had found Verbruggen's killer sooner ... then ... then my father would still be alive today."

DeKok stared at the young man. He would never admit it, but Dervoor's words hurt, more than he would have expected. But his face remained a mask.

"Your mother," he said soothingly, "asked you to talk to me ... not to accuse me. You must keep in mind that not everybody has the same drive, spirit and capacity for work that your father had ... otherwise he would not have been such a great man."

Dervoor bowed his head and for a long time he remained silent. His face regained a more normal color. Then he looked up. His blue eyes were calm.

"I'm sorry," he spoke, repentance in his voice. "That wasn't fair. But the thought that my father is gone ... that I never again can talk with him, see him ... it just makes me ... eh, rebellious."

DeKok sighed.

"I promise you that I will do my best." It sounded trite and he knew it. "It's not an easy case," he continued. "There is little to go on. Your father's death has introduced a new aspect in the death of Verbruggen. I have to rethink my position. The motive reaches farther than the death of the banker."

"I know him," said Dervoor.

"Who?"

"The killer."

Both Vledder and DeKok looked up in surprise.

"You *know* him?" asked DeKok, disbelief in his voice.

"I'll never forget it, I was still a boy," said young Dervoor. "I played soccer in those days, for Ajax. Junior Division, of course. I dreamed of being a star until a knee injury put an end to *that* dream. One day, after training, a man was standing near the exit from the stadium. Apparently he had been waiting for me. He came toward me and asked if I was the son of Jean-Paul Dervoor … the big man at Electronics International."

"And then?"

"I said, yes, that was my father."

"What happened next?" asked DeKok with bated breath.

"He said something like that it was time that someone should stop him permanently. He looked at me for a while and then asked me if I knew who that someone might be. He then pointed at himself and said: 'That someone is me.' Then he left."

"What did you do?" DeKok had a feeling of deja-vu.

"I told my father about it, that night."

"And?"

"He laughed and said: 'Pete doesn't have the nerve.' We never discussed it again, after that."

12

Vledder interrupted enthusiastically.

"We got him," he proclaimed happily. "That's the guy we're looking for. No question about it. It's the link between both murders."

Jean Baptiste Dervoor looked with surprise at the young Inspector. He had hardly noticed him until now.

"He's an older man," he explained, "about the same age as my father. Maybe a little older."

Vledder gestured toward DeKok.

"We have heard about that guy. He spoke in almost exactly the same way about Verbruggen."

Jean was taken aback.

"You know him?"

DeKok shook his head.

"Verbruggen used to visit a prostitute. She told us about him. We don't know who he is."

Dervoor sighed.

"I don't know who he is, either. But when we heard about my father's death, I thought about him immediately. I asked Mother if she knew any Pete in connection with my father. But the name did not mean anything to her."

"But you asked your father, as well, didn't you?" asked De-

Kok. "Apparently he knew at once who you were talking about."

"He knew. And I had the distinct impression that it wasn't the first time he had heard the threat. But he acted so nonchalant, so light hearted, that I never asked any further."

A new Inspector, Raap, entered the room and approached DeKok's desk. He carried a gray, plastic bag over one shoulder. He swung it on top of DeKok's desk.

DeKok greeted him with a smile.

"What's all this, Frans?" he asked.

"The stuff from the corpse ... that Dervoor. From the lab." He waved in Vledder's direction. "Sir, there, didn't want to ride with the meat wagon and over the radio he asked me to do it."

"You were about?"

"Yes, I happened to be in the neighborhood of Mill's Quarter."

"You didn't mind?"

"Ach, no trouble, really."

DeKok pointed at the bag.

"Did you find any letters?"

"No, I checked all his pockets after they undressed him at the lab. Just a wallet, some money, credit cards and a folder with car papers. No letters." He paused. "Oh, yes, Kruger asked me to tell you that he found another note under the Pierrot with the same text. He took it with him to check for prints."

DeKok merely nodded.

Inspector Raap put a hand in an inside pocket and produced a pistol. It was a heavily decorated, small weapon with a mother-of-pearl handle. He turned it around. The initials JRS were engraved on both sides.

"How did you get that?" asked DeKok.

"It was in the right hand outside pocket of his jacket."

DeKok accepted the weapon.

"You found it on Dervoor?" he asked, surprised.

"Yes," nodded Raap. "Better be careful. It's still loaded. One in the chamber and five in the magazine. 7.65 caliber, just like our small Police-FN."

DeKok showed the weapon to Jean Baptiste.

"Have you ever seen this before?"

Young Dervoor looked pale as he shook his head.

"It doesn't belong to my father," he said softly, almost whispering. "Father ... Father never carried a weapon."

* * *

After Jean Baptiste Dervoor had left and Frans Raap had also taken his leave, DeKok again picked up the pistol. The beautiful weapon intrigued him. He looked at Vledder who was busy on his computer.

"Why?" asked DeKok. "Why would a man who never carried a weapon, according to his son, and who has never been in the service and probably doesn't know how such a thing works, suddenly have a pistol in his pocket?"

Vledder grunted while he finished some entries.

"As a precaution," he suggested. "Because he was afraid ... feared an attack."

"Afraid of what ... of who?"

"An attacker," answered Vledder. "An attack from a man, or woman, he expected to meet."

"So Jean Dervoor was keeping an appointment," mused DeKok. "Just like his friend, Verbruggen, ten days ago. An appointment with his killer." DeKok stood up and leaned over Vledder's desk. "And *he* was aware of the danger," he added.

"That's why he carried a weapon," agreed Vledder.

"But yet," said DeKok, staring into the distance. "And yet he went." He brought his attention back to Vledder. "There were no letters with the corpse of Verbruggen, either, were there?"

"No."

"But Verbruggen had received a letter ... that Sunday. The letter that directed him to Mill's Quarter ... to Carla's apartment. I wonder if Jean Dervoor also received such a letter ... and if so, what became of both letters?"

Vledder grimaced.

"The killer must have taken them back, after the killing."

"Why?"

Vledder shrugged impatiently.

"You'll have to ask the killer."

"Because," said DeKok, ignoring the interruption, "the letters contained a clue."

"Oh, yes," mocked Vledder. "Then why did he leave the text behind?"

"The baptismal text?"

"Yes, you know very well what I mean."

"Well, the text was *not* left for us."

"For who then?"

DeKok looked grim.

"For his next victim."

The phone rang on DeKok's desk. DeKok ignored it and out of habit Vledder reached over to answer. A few moments later he hung up.

"Little Lowee is downstairs."

"Well, tell them to send him up."

Vledder dialed and repeated the instruction. A few minutes later Lowee's mousy little face peeked around the edge of the door. With a smile of satisfaction he entered the room and approached DeKok.

"I ain't gotta lotta time. Blue Jake is lookin' out for me, but that guy drink like a fish."

DeKok laughed.

"You should get a teetotaler for behind the bar," he advised.

Lowee grinned.

"Ain't got much of them inna Quarter. Good thing too," he added, "iffen there was too much of them, I coulda close up."

"Well, you still always have your fencing business," said Vledder maliciously.

Lowee stiffened.

"What's that noise?" he asked DeKok.

"What noise?" asked DeKok, winking.

With a grin the small barkeeper pulled a chair close to De-Kok's desk and sat down.

"Lass time you was at my place," he said in a confidential whisper, "you wants to know iffen Jimmy Munk writes them letters."

"Yes," said DeKok, "I asked you if he was still in the business."

"I ask aroun', you knows and yep, he still do. Makin' a mint, 'e do. Musta be plenty of rich fish that wanna pay 'im to keep his mouth shut. He done got a condo atta beach. An' he gotta big place in Spain."

"How do you know?"

Lowee smiled triumphantly.

"Uncle Cor ... Cor the Carpenter. The place in Spain is sorta run down, you knows and Jimmy ask Cor to go fix it. Jimmy don't speak no Spanish and he wanna have somebody he can talk to."

"So, he asked Uncle Cor."

"Got it. Uncle Cor gets the loot for the job and he can stay there with his kids and his old lady."

DeKok nodded. It was clear that Jimmy had more money

than he should have.

"And what about this educated young lady he's supposed to have?"

"Carla ... Carla Heeten is her moniker. Nice little place in Mill's Quarter and ..." Lowee stopped suddenly. He looked at De-Kok with wide open mouth. "But ... but that's where them two geezers done been killed. That's *your* case, ain't it?"

DeKok laughed heartily. He thoroughly enjoyed the expression on Lowee's face.

"You think Jimmy is financing all that from blackmail?" he asked, returning to business.

Lowee looked offended.

"What else?"

"From the money Carla brings in ..." began DeKok.

Lowee interrupted.

"Carla's loot ... Pah, nebbish. That ain't nothing what with the other takes." He shook his head. "Nah, ain't never seen a broad get real mullah from hooking. Besides," he added, "this Carla got 'er own little toys, you know, got some stud onna side."

"What do you mean?"

"Well," grimaced Lowee, "a stud, some muscle guy, you knows, somebody she can do it with, and free, see."

"Love?"

"Nah, sex, what else."

"You know him?"

"Sure I knows 'im. Beau Robbie they calls him. You knows a guy that's always lookin' after his own self. Real narc ... nars ..."

"Narcissist," supplied DeKok.

"Yep, that's it. Full of hisself, see."

"Do you know his real name?"

"No," said Lowee, thinking hard, "No, not iffen you ask me

like that. But I can find out for you, don't you worry about that, DeKok. I thinks he's a wise guy these days."

"Why do you say that?"

"His wheels is too rich for his blood, for one. Got one of them Eyetalian jobs. Drove it smack inna canal oncet. Guess who was sitting inna car with him?"

"Who?"

"Jimmy Munk. Whadda you think of *that*?"

DeKok looked surprised.

"Carla's ... eh, friend."

Lowee nodded complacently, satisfied with the effect of his words.

"Yessir, both of them in that itty bitty car. Costa lotta loot, car like that. He also bought a piece."

"Who?"

"Robbie."

"What kind of weapon?"

"Revolver ... nine millimeter Smith & Wesson." When it came to technical details about the tools of his trade, Lowee managed to loose his accent altogether.

"A nine millimeter," asked DeKok. "Are you sure?"

"Sure, I's sure. Appie the Ace done tole me so hisself. He got it for 'im. Special order, you see."

13

DeKok had tired feet.

With his trousers rolled up to his knees he gingerly lowered his hairy legs into a bucket of warm water. An effervescent foot powder bubbled up from between his toes. Bent over and with a pain distorted face he massaged his calves. Thousands of tiny devils were using his legs as a pincushion for their malicious tridents. The pain also made him melancholy. He knew too well what it meant. It meant he was at a total loss and far, very far removed from a solution in the case. Whenever an investigation went wrong, when he could not find a thread, when he was without a single clue, the little devils would attack his legs. He called it "tired feet," but the pain extended from the tips of his toes to the knees and had a paralyzing effect. Years ago he had been told that there was no physical reason for feeling the way he did. It was all psychosomatic. With a small part of his brain he acknowledged that, but the pain was just as real and he was powerless to control it.

He glanced up at his wife who looked at him with a compassionate smile.

"You want some more warm water?" she asked, concern in her voice.

"My feet aren't pig's trotters," he groused. "I already feel like the meat is just about to fall off the bone. Throw some vegetables in the bucket and you'll have a good, hearty soup."

Mrs. DeKok merely smiled to herself. She knew about the pain, and its causes, better than most. She knew her husband's moods and knew that his crotchety mood was the result of his work, not his feet.

"Getting nowhere?" she asked sweetly.

The gray sleuth sighed deeply. He lifted his left leg and let the water drip back in the bucket. He examined his foot carefully, but could find no sign of trauma. The foot looked normal, big and a bit flat-footed, but normal.

"I've been running after Appie the Ace most of the day," he said. "Every time I thought I had run him to earth, he had just left."

"Who's that ... Appie the Ace."

"An old street gambler. Used to make a lot of money with three-card-monte, but for the last few years he's been in the illegal weapons business."

"And why do you want him? What has he to do with the murders?"

DeKok shook his head.

"I don't know, but he sold a revolver to a young man, Beau Robbie. Robbie has some connection to the call-girl in the apartment in Mill's Quarter, where both victims were killed. And the murders happened with a revolver of the same caliber as was bought by Robbie."

Mrs. DeKok gave her husband a searching look.

"And this Robbie is a murderer?"

DeKok smiled with clenched teeth.

"Nobody is born a killer. Life determines who becomes one. Nobody can tell ..." He paused. Another smile fled across his face. "Apart from their gruesome work, I have another complaint about murderers ... they all look so normal, just like anybody else."

"Are they really so ... so, eh ..."

"Human?"

Mrs. DeKok shook her head.

"No, that's not the word I was looking for. I don't think murderers are quite human."

"Murder is a typically human business."

They remained silent for a while.

"And this Robbie, does he have a normal face? Does he look like anybody else?"

"I don't know," said DeKok. "I've never seen his face."

The telephone on the sideboard rang out. Mrs. DeKok looked at her husband.

"Are you home?" she asked. A look passed between them which could only be interpreted by people who had been long and happily married.

The Inspector pointed at the bucket with a martyred face.

"Just find out who it is and what they want. I'll decide then," he said.

Mrs. DeKok picked up the receiver and listened.

"He has tired feet," she said into the phone. "He has his feet in the water right now ... Good ... I'll tell him."

She replaced the receiver.

"Vledder?" asked DeKok.

"Of course," said his wife. "Some detective you are. Couldn't you tell from what I said?"

"No, dear. There's isn't a male detective in the world who will ever completely understand a woman. Least of all his own wife."

She smiled tenderly.

"Yes, it was Vledder. He called from the station. A certain

Mr. Broos called to say he was ready to pay fifty thousand guilders."

"When?"

"Tonight."

"Where?"

"I don't know. Dick didn't say and I didn't ask. He said he was on the way here and I told him fine. He'll be here shortly."

* * *

DeKok hoisted himself into the aged VW. His face was more cheerful. The footbath had done its work. Psychosomatic, or not, he thought. He smiled at his partner as they drove away.

"Did Broos come to the station house?"

"No, he phoned. I was just about to leave. Lucky I got the call at all."

"What did he say?"

"He just said that he was going to deliver fifty thousand guilders at ten o'clock tonight."

"Where?"

"In a bicycle and pedestrian tunnel near the Dovecote Metro station. He was instructed to park his car at the Metro station and to proceed on foot." Subconsciously Vledder spoke in the formalized bureaucratic language so beloved of report writers. "He is to proceed in the direction of the tall apartment buildings. Someone will accost him in the tunnel and take possession of the funds, which are to be in denominations of one hundred guilders."

"Hundreds, eh?"

"Yes."

"How did Broos get that many one hundred guilder notes on short notice?"

"Oh, he had them ready. He was told a few days ago to have

138

the funds available in the specified denominations."

"He never told us that."

Vledder grunted.

"Apparently he wanted to keep us out of it. He thought that would be safer. Only today he decided to notify the police ... that is, us."

"A bit late," growled DeKok.

"You can say that again," sighed Vledder. "He called after the shift change and everybody was already on the street. You know how it is."

DeKok nodded. Warmoes Street station, more than any other police station, usually had its entire force on the street. The crew in the station house normally consisted of the Watch Commander, some clerks and the occasional detective who might come in to write a report. There were seldom any reserves available in the station and to get help from other stations would have meant endless red tape and insufferable delays.

"Well," continued Vledder. "We'll just have to manage between us. What time is it?"

The VW had no clock. DeKok looked at his watch.

"About nine thirty-five," he said.

"Less than half an hour. We'll just make it." Vledder glanced at the radio. "Not enough time to contact the Dovecote police and ask for back-up," he said.

DeKok was not interested. Mobile radios simply did not exist in his world.

"Is Broos really carrying fifty thousand?" There was astonishment in the older man's voice.

"Well, I *did* advise him to keep the money in his safe and to fill a suitcase with newspapers."

"And?"

"He said," grinned Vledder, "that he would take my advice

under advisement. He didn't sound very nice, nor cooperative."

DeKok was irate.

"Actually," he said furiously, "we should just leave a guy like that to his own devices. If it wasn't for those two murders, I'd be tempted to turn around and go home."

Vledder laughed out loud.

"Sure you would," he said. "I can just imagine you walking away from *any* crime. Besides, think of Article 28 of the Police Manual: *to assist those who are in need of such assistance as may be warranted.* And Broos is in need of assistance, whether he knows it or not."

"Yes," grumbled DeKok, "in the States they write it on their cruisers. *Preserve and protect,* or something like that."

"That's right," said Vledder, "that's in Los Angeles. How did you know? You don't watch television."

DeKok did not answer. He was still nursing a grudge.

"I suppose we have to protect Broos and preserve his money," he said after a while. Then he snorted. "But really, a guy like this Broos ... he really doesn't deserve our help. He has seen with his own eyes what happened to Dervoor ... after some hassle, I finally get him to admit he also received threatening letters ... he eventually promises cooperation ... and then, at the last moment he tells us he's going to pay anyway. What sort of character *is* that?" He paused and took a deep breath.

"How did he receive the information?" he asked in a calmer tone of voice.

"By phone."

"Anything to go on? Voice? Background noise?"

"I don't know," said Vledder. "I simply didn't have a chance to interrogate him at length. He told me as quickly and tersely as possible and hung up."

DeKok pointed through the windshield.

"Dovecote Metro Station," he remarked. "Just park anywhere."

Vledder glanced at his partner.

"You know that Broos has instructions to park there. Don't
you think our police car will be a bit obvious?" He gestured
around. "Look at all the lights."

DeKok grinned maliciously.

"Just park it anywhere. Nobody will believe that the Amsterdam Police operates dilapidated cars like this. Besides, " he
added, "I want to walk from here to the tunnel. Perhaps we'll discover why this particular spot was picked."

Vledder parked the car across from the modern terminal.
They exited the car and slammed the doors.

DeKok looked around. It was very quiet. The Metro station
seemed deserted. In the distance the tall apartment buildings were
clearly delineated against the light of the moon. DeKok thought
about the difficulties involved in building such tall structures. For
centuries the height of buildings in the Netherlands had been se-
verely limited by the soft, wet ground caused by the fact that most
of Holland is below sea level. A rule of thumb used to be that for
every foot up, the foundations had to go two feet down. Many
short-cuts, some more or less successful than others, had been de-
vised. The Royal Palace in Amsterdam was built on 13,659 poles.
A church in Delft was constructed on top of a meters thick layer
of cowhides. The spire towers more than 320 feet in the air and
over the years the church has started to lean. Its angle is almost as
acute as the leaning Tower of Pisa, but *this* tower is made from
brick. Modern techniques and power tools had solved the ancient
problems and skyscrapers are almost as common in the Netherlands as elsewhere. After another look, they walked in the direction of the looming apartment buildings.

The evening air was chilly and a raw wind blustered across

the foot path. DeKok pulled up his collar and pulled his hat down over his forehead.

The pedestrian and bicycle tunnel was about fifty yards from the station. It was about fifty feet long and pierced the dike underneath a road under construction.

Their steps sounded hollow in the concrete tube. To the right somebody had written a feminist slogan on the wall in vibrant red colors. *Give us less men and more sun*, read DeKok. He smiled.

At the end of the tunnel, the road split. A deserted road led to the left, toward the apartment building. The bicycle path continued to the right into the distance, apparently paralleling the dike above. DeKok stopped.

From around here, he mused, the receiver should appear. There were only a few possibilities. He, or she, would have to come by foot, by bicycle, or by motorbike. There was no room for a car. He just could not visualize the man or woman. It was all too strange, out of reach.

He searched in his pocket and found a peppermint. Thoughtfully he put it in his mouth. He would have liked to have some backup, but Vledder was right. There had been no time. Silently he cursed the stupidity of Broos. If he had called them sooner, they could have made preparations. Just Vledder and himself had little chance of success. There was also no way to protect Broos while he was inside the tunnel.

Actually the place was not ideal from the blackmailer's point of view, he thought. If he had been able to get enough help, he could have closed off both sides of the tunnel and that would have been that.

To the right of the tunnel, in the bushes, he found a footpath consisting of trampled earth. It was apparently created by pedestrians who, for one reason or another, wanted to cross to the other side of the dike, without using the tunnel. DeKok approached the informal path and climbed up in the loose sand. Vledder followed.

From the top of the dike one had a perfect view of the brightly lit Metro station. From this spot they could also see the entrance to the tunnel.

"We better wait here," said DeKok. "From here we can see both sides of the tunnel and can run down on anyone." He looked at his watch. "It should happen within the next five minutes." He looked at Vledder. "Do you know what kind of car Broos is driving? Would you recognize it in the parking lot?"

"No," said Vledder, "because I had no chance to ask him. I'm sure it's an expensive car. If you can so easily pay out fifty thousand ..." He stopped talking and pointed in the direction of the Metro station. "There, next to our car ... a black Cadillac."

Tensely the Inspectors watched. After a few moments a short, compact man came out of the Cadillac. He was dressed in a long, black overcoat, a white scarf and there was a homburg on his head. He carried a briefcase in one hand.

"Broos?" asked Vledder.

DeKok nodded.

Broos walked down the footpath toward the tunnel. The lights of the station made a long shadow in front of him, as if pointing the way.

It seemed an eternity before Broos had covered the distance. It seemed he stopped after every step and looked behind him. Finally he entered the tunnel. They could clearly hear his steps echo against the walls. DeKok listened intently, expecting an interruption in the cadence. But that did not happen.

Suddenly a young man ran from the tunnel, dressed in a blue jogging suit.

For a moment DeKok froze.

"Marius!"

14

Vledder ran down the dike.

For another instant DeKok stood as if nailed to the ground. Then he, too, moved. With a short, surprisingly fast sprint, he overtook Vledder and took him by the shoulder. He lost his balance in the attempt and pulled Vledder down with him. Together they rolled down the rest of the slope.

Vledder stood up first. Then he helped his partner up.

DeKok felt several parts of his legs and arms and concluded nothing was broken and that he was generally intact. But his hat had disappeared. He looked around and saw it in some bramble bushes. Gingerly he retrieved his faithful companion.

Vledder brushed off his clothes.

"Everything OK?" he asked.

DeKok grimaced.

"I think so, unless I've overlooked the odd bone, here or there."

Vledder laughed, relieved.

"But why did you stop me?" asked Vledder. "If you had let me go, I would have caught him."

DeKok shook his head.

"That would not have achieved anything. You see, Marius did not have the briefcase."

Vledder gave him a skeptical look.

"He didn't?"

"I saw that at once," smiled DeKok. "Apart from the blue jogging suit, it was just about the first thing I noticed." He shook some sand from a sleeve. "They took us for a ride."

"How's that?"

"I think that Marius has a regular routine. I think he *always* passes here about this time."

"Are you saying that Marius has nothing to do with all this?"

"Yes," answered DeKok, "that's exactly what I think. I'm convinced that somebody has pulled our leg." He replaced his hat after having brushed it carefully. "Remember the visit to Mrs. Kolfs, here in Dovecote? Marius came home at about this time, in a jogging suit. Well, Herb Way is practically around the corner from here."

"But the blackmailer must have known that," protested Vledder.

"Sure," agreed DeKok. "He knew. I guess that the black-mailer didn't trust our Mr. Broos very much. As you know, I talked with him at some length at Wadden Street station after he discovered the corpse. I'm sure the blackmailer knows about that. Although he cannot know the exact subject of the conversation, he must keep the possibility in mind that Broos told all."

"Nice," grumped Vledder.

"Isn't it? The blackmailer took no risk, whatsoever. He carefully selected the time and place to confuse us."

"Marius ... ten o'clock," said Vledder, stating the obvious.

"Exactly," said DeKok seriously. "When I saw Marius run from the tunnel I froze for just a moment, but then I realized he did not have the briefcase and I concluded almost at once that the boy could not be connected with the case. As I said, he did not have the briefcase, but also ... Marius is not the type ... he's no

146

blackmailer. A young man who rejects all claims to a large inheritance ... does not commit blackmail for a measly fifty thousand."

"And that's why you stopped me."

The gray sleuth laughed merrily.

"It's been a while since I last played 'tag,' but the old skills are still there." Suddenly he slapped his forehead. "Broos," he cried out, upset, "Broos!" he repeated. "We've forgotten all about Broos."

They ran toward the tunnel and there they found Broos. He stood about halfway down the tunnel, a strange look on his face and a briefcase in his hand.

* * *

"What do we know about Pete?"

Vledder looked up from his computer.

"You mean the old man who promised to stop both Verbruggen and Dervoor?"

"*That* Pete," confirmed DeKok.

Vledder hit a few keys on his keyboard and turned his chair toward DeKok.

"Well," he began, "it's almost certain that Blonde Hennie and young Dervoor met the same person. Believe me, I've tried, but so far I have no positive identification. From the descriptions I have ordered a police drawing and both Hennie and Jean Baptiste have looked through our Rogues Gallery. No luck. I asked those two to discuss their respective meetings with each other, but ..."

"Why?"

"I was hoping that they could remind each other of something they had overlooked. I mean, one could have seen the color of the eyes and the other ..."

"Yes, yes," interrupted DeKok. "in other words, we've no clues."

"No, both Hennie and young Dervoor agreed that he was a well-dressed man, who spoke a very distinguished kind of Dutch, without an accent. That's about it."

"Oh, well," said DeKok with a sigh, "at least that narrows it down. There can only be a few hundred thousand people like that in the country."

"What else can I do?" asked Vledder. "I've thought about circulating the sketch, but it only vaguely describes an older man, about seven or eight years ago."

"I know," said DeKok. "What about the letters?"

Vledder looked more cheerful.

"*Those* I have." He pulled open a drawer of his desk and at the same time did something to his computer. "Ad Dishoven dug them up for me. It took more than an hour to sort through everything, but," he added, slapping a thick folder with his hand, "this is Jimmy Munk for the last ten years."

"Results?"

Vledder handed over the folder, while he watched the first sheets appearing in the output basket of his printer.

"The letters to Broos are identical with letters from earlier in Jimmy's career. He seems to have used a kind of form letter. Just the names, places and circumstances are different. Here is the result," Vledder said, as he pushed over some sheets that had been produced by the printer. "As you'll see, the likelihood that the letters are from the same author is almost 100% percent. Except for the typewriter. He's switched typewriters over the years, but even that can be an indication. Hardly anyone uses typewriters anymore. It's usually computer printers that cannot easily be individually identified."

"A different letter type?" asked DeKok, concentrating on the least technical aspect.

"Yes," answered Vledder. "The computer identified at least ten distinct differences in the way the letters were formed, as well as in the overall type face."

"And what about Verbruggen's letters?"

Vledder's face fell.

"No match. They're totally different ... in content, style and letter type." He shook his head. "You said it yourself, Verbruggen's letters are not really blackmail letters. They're *threatening* letters. They just make an announcement, but there is no follow-up ... no demand for money ... no alternative."

DeKok shook his head angrily.

"And yet, there *has* to be a connection. Carla's flat and her relationship with Jimmy Munk are central to both murders. There is no other way ... it is more than just coincidence."

"There's no such thing as a coincidence." Vledder quoted one of DeKok's own maxims.

"True," conceded DeKok. "And the charade in the tunnel in Dovecote also proves that the blackmailer is rather completely informed about Verbruggen's private life and that of his children. If you consider that Marius hasn't had any contact with his father for years, we can also be certain that the blackmailer also knows all about Mrs. Kolfs."

For a long time DeKok stared morosely into the distance. Then he stood up and started to pace through the room. Without really seeing the obstacles, he subconsciously avoided them all. Chairs, desks, outstretched legs, waste baskets and file cabinets seemed not to exist for him. His hands were folded on his back and his head was bowed. After a while he stopped in front of the window and stared out over the rooftops of the Red Light District. Suddenly he turned and pointed at Vledder.

"You get hold of Jimmy Munk. Tell him anything you like,

149

but make sure that he's in this station no later than eight o'clock tonight. And hold him for as long as possible."

"Then what?"

DeKok held up an admonishing finger.

"As soon as he gets here, you put him in the waiting room and then you call me at the police station in Seadike."

"Seadike? Why Seadike?"

DeKok smirked mysteriously.

"You should know ... Jimmy Munk has a beach place there."

* * *

Handy Henkie moped in the passenger seat of the car which was in the wrong gear on its way to Seadike. DeKok was driving. Henkie closed his eyes in resignation. But after a while the bucking and bumping of the car forced him to open his eyes. He preferred to know it when the final bump came. In his mind he had resigned himself to not surviving this unexpected ride. DeKok cheerfully admitted that he was the worst driver in Amsterdam, possibly in all of the Netherlands. In order to hide his nervousness, Henkie began to speak.

"I don't like it, Mr. DeKok, I just don't want to." There was a rebellious tone in his whine. "Despite our good relations, I don't want to do it again. You know I've retired."

The gray sleuth grinned between clenched teeth.

"You used to do it for your own profit, now you're doing it in the cause of justice."

Henkie snorted.

"Justice ... who believes them fairy tales anymore."

"I do," answered DeKok simply.

Henkie, once known as Handy Henkie the burglar, thought

150

about that. He was now a respected instrument maker, but he had been arrested and convicted several times for burglary. DeKok finally convinced him to change his life of crime to an honest occupation. Over the years he had worked with DeKok on a number of illegal break-ins. DeKok seldom allowed the letter of the law to stand between himself and the apprehension of a murderer. Henkie had supplied DeKok with an ingenious instrument of his own invention and with it DeKok was able to open just about any lock and had frequently done so. This time he needed Henkie, however. Despite his objections, Henkie was ready to help his old friend.

"You know, DeKok," said Henkie in a didactic tone, "you're a good cop. I'll be the last to contradict that. But, if Justice needs an ex-burglar to function, there's something rotten in Denmark. It just ain't right."

DeKok listened seriously. Henkie had almost completely lost his thieves language and tried to use as many multi-syllable words as possible. No doubt the influence of his daughter, thought DeKok. Not too long ago, DeKok had been instrumental in solving a case where Henkie's daughter had been the prime suspect.* No doubt, thought DeKok, there were now also grandchildren who would benefit from Henkie's new-found respectability and vocabulary.

"You're right, Henkie. There's something wrong with our system of justice. As upholders of the Law we have less and less room to maneuver ... more and more restrictions. The real crooks, and there seem to be more of those as time goes on, are too well protected. But for the victims there seems to be less and less protection ... less Justice."

"And that's why I gotta do a job for you?"

---

* See: *DeKok and the Deadly Accord.*

"No, I'll do the break-in myself," smiled DeKok.

"You still have my little present?"

"Wouldn't be without it. Used it several times."

"Then what am I doing here?"

DeKok had no time to answer. He braked hard and to his right another car stopped just as suddenly, barely missing De-Kok's car. The driver of the other car pointed at his forehead in the universal gesture indicating idiocy.

"You ran a red light!" yelled Henkie accusingly.

With a great deal of crashing from the abused gears and total disregard for the clutch, DeKok coaxed the VW into motion.

"What was your question?" he asked, as if nothing had happened.

"What you need me for?" repeated Henkie, wiping cold sweat from his forehead.

At the end of the street DeKok parked the car half on and half off the sidewalk. He pointed at a large condominium.

"That's our destination. Unit 705. That's where Jimmy Munk lives."

"Who's that?"

"A blackmailer. I think he may be responsible for the death of at least two people. That's why I want to know what kind of papers he keeps in the house."

Handy Henkie grinned.

"Go ahead. I'll wait here for you."

DeKok opened the car door and turned to his passenger.

"You don't think I took you away from the bosom of your family, just for a little trip to Seadike, did you? No, I'm sure that Jimmy keeps his records in a safe and for *that* I need you."

The ex-burglar rubbed his fingertips together.

"I don't know, DeKok. I don't know if I still have the touch, you know."

"I'm sure you haven't lost it."

The main entrance was no problem. It took DeKok less than ten seconds. Boldly they took the elevator to the seventh floor. There was a long corridor with wall-to-wall carpeting. They stopped in front of 705 and again DeKok produced the little brass cylinder that hid so many secrets and unlocked so many doors.

Henkie watched with admiration as it took DeKok less than half a minute to open the door.

"You're good, DeKok. If you weren't a cop, we could go in business together."

"Would you go back to it, then?"

"With you ... like a shot."

DeKok did not answer, but entered the luxurious condominium. As they crossed the foyer, Henkie tapped him on the shoulder.

"Don't we need a look-out?" he whispered.

"No problem," said DeKok conversationally. "Jimmy is in Warmoes Street, listening to Vledder's stories."

"You're a born crook," whistled Henkie with admiration.

DeKok accepted that as high praise. From the foyer they entered a living room. DeKok aimed the beam of his flashlight around the interior. The furniture was impressive, excessive. The entire space seemed crammed with fragile chairs, tables, cabinets and chests.

"Looks like a doll's house," growled Henkie.

"Louis Seize ... Queen Anne ... Biedemaier ... Chippendale."

"What?"

"An expensive collection. What do you figure?"

"I wouldn't give you a wooden nickel for it," snorted Henkie.

From the living room they reached a bedroom. A large four-poster bed dominated the room. In the far corner they saw a huge, steel safe. DeKok played the beam across the safe.

"Look familiar?"

Handy Henkie nodded slowly.

"Old French case. I've opened one or two, in my time." He looked at DeKok. "A long time ago."

"Just try it, Henkie," said DeKok with an encouraging smile.

The ex-burglar took off his jacket and revealed a broad belt, set with stitched-on pockets. Each pocket contained an instrument of some kind. He took off the belt and placed it on the floor, next to the safe. Then he knelt down in front of the heavy steel door and carefully felt for the ribbed surface of the combination dial.

DeKok watched tensely. It was not the first time he had seen Henkie at his old craft, but it always fascinated him. Meanwhile Henkie's face was devoid of expression as he carefully turned the lock first one way and then the other. One ear leaned against the door. His devotion and dedication to the task at hand was total. DeKok had disappeared as far as Henkie was concerned.

"How's it going?"

Henkie turned around, sweat beaded his forehead.

"A bit tougher than I thought," he sighed. "I must have worked with older, less refined models."

DeKok looked at his watch. It was almost nine o'clock. He wondered how long Vledder would be able to keep Jimmy at the station house.

Suddenly Henkie cried out.

"Got ye!"

He turned the heavy brass wheel and pulled. The heavy door opened with deceptive ease. DeKok placed a hand on his shoulder.

"Real class, Henkie."

Henkie beamed with pride.

Three-ring binders were arranged in orderly rows inside the safe.

"This what you're looking for?" asked Henkie.

DeKok nodded and knelt down in front of the safe.

"I think that Jimmy knows more about business in the Netherlands than the IRS."

He picked up a binder marked with the letter 'V' on the spine.

He flipped through it, looking for Verbruggen's name. There was a lot of information, complete with newspaper cuttings and a photo. He showed the photo to Henkie.

"This is one of the men who was killed."

He replaced the binder and pulled out one marked with 'D.'

Dervoor was also represented by an exhaustive biography and supporting documents.

For a moment he fought the urge to confiscate the binders and take them with him. With a sigh he replaced the 'D' binder as well. There was no way, he reflected. There was no way he would ever be able to explain how he gained possession of the binders. He glanced through a few more binders, then he looked at Henkie with a sad look on his face.

"You can close it again," he said resignedly.

Henkie was shocked.

"Close it up? Don't you want to pick something out?"

Slowly DeKok shook his head as he laboriously climbed back to his feet.

"Justice has it own methods, Henkie ... and even I don't always understand them."

The ex-burglar shrugged. He pushed close the heavy door, turned the brass wheel and adjusted the combination lock. He pulled a rag from a pocket and wiped every surface he had touched. Then he stood up, pulled his tool belt around him and picked up his jacket.

"Too bad about the wasted effort," he said, pulling on his jacket.

DeKok briefly placed an arm around Henkie's shoulder.

"Never mind. Thank you, anyway."

For a few more moments they stood silently in front of the safe, as if saying goodbye. Then they turned to leave. Suddenly they froze in place. They heard the lock of the front door click, followed by the sound of footsteps.

DeKok pulled Henkie back.

"Hide under the bed," he whispered urgently. "As soon as the coast is clear, take off. Wait for me by the car."

Henkie disappeared. DeKok ran a hand through his hair and pulled loose his necktie. Then he entered the living room. At almost the same time the light was switched on.

DeKok blinked his eyes and looked at Carla Heeten. There was an astonished look on her face. Her hand was still on the light switch.

15

"What ... eh, what are *you* doing here?"

DeKok laughed sheepishly. He rubbed his old hat with the sleeve of his raincoat. He was obviously embarrassed.

"I think he got away," he said finally.

"Who ... what?"

"A burglar."

"A burglar?" repeated Carla.

"Yes," nodded DeKok. He straightened out his necktie. "There was an anonymous tip that a burglary was planned for Jimmy Munk's condo in Seadike. They were after some antiques."

"Antiques?"

"Yes, at least that was the message. At first I was going to contact the Seadike police, but I thought, before they understand what's happening, it may be too late. So I came myself."

"But the front door was locked."

DeKok ignored that.

"You saw nobody in the hall?"

"No."

"Then he may still be inside." He took Carla by an arm and pulled her into the kitchen. Reluctantly she followed.

"Are there any other rooms?" asked DeKok.

"The bedroom."

"I just came from there."

"The guest room."

"Where is that?"

With a frightened face Carla led the way. From the kitchen to the foyer and from there to a small room with a single bed. De-Kok took his time. While he searched the bed thoroughly he heard the front door slam shut. A silent sigh of relief escaped him.

"There he goes," cried Carla.

DeKok stormed out of the room. Halfway down the foyer he stopped.

"It's useless," he said. "He's gone."

Casually he sauntered back to the living room and lowered himself into one of the fragile chairs. He looked dejected.

"Is anything missing?" asked DeKok.

Carla shrugged shapely shoulders.

"I can't tell. Jimmy always has the place packed with all sorts of things."

DeKok merely nodded in resignation.

"I would advise Jimmy to contact the Seadike police as soon as possible and report this."

"Did you see him?" she asked.

"Who?"

"The burglar."

There was a painful look on DeKok's face as he rubbed his chin. He seemed lost in thought.

"I felt him," he said after a long pause. "For just a moment … then he slipped away. It was pitch dark. I would not be able to describe him." He stood up and walked over to a beautifully decorated full-length mirror. He took a comb from a back pocket and combed his gray hair into a semblance of respectability. Because of his habit of wearing a hat most of the time, the hair was unruly and the effort was mostly wasted. Then he turned around. His expression had changed. It frightened Carla.

"Why ... why were you not in your apartment last Wednesday to meet Mr. Broos?"

Carla took a step back, felt for a chair behind her and slowly sat down. She remained silent. She avoided his eyes.

"Why weren't you there?" DeKok insisted.

Carla Heeten swallowed.

"I wasn't supposed to be," she said hoarsely.

"Who told you that?"

Suddenly she looked pale.

DeKok took her by the shoulders and shook her gently.

"Answer me," he commanded.

Carla swallowed again. Her lips trembled.

"Mr. Schaap ... Mr. Schaap told me to stay away."

* * *

Vledder smirked.

"She believed you?"

DeKok nodded, smiling.

"Especially when she heard the front door slam shut. It was beautiful." He paused. "I had a lot more trouble with Henkie. I better send a nice bouquet to his wife. It may help bring me back in Henkie's good graces."

"Why?"

"Because we were surprised by Carla. Henkie wasn't too thrilled with that. It scared him. Henkie is a professional, a perfectionist. He blamed me for insufficient preparation. 'You shoulda cased the joint,' he said. Also, he felt that the whole expedition was a waste of time."

"Was it?"

"Henkie thought so."

"Was the safe empty?"

"Oh, no," answered DeKok. "On the contrary. Rows upon rows of binders with what looked like complete documentation about some of the most influential people in our society ... hobbies ... connections ... powers, weaknesses ... especially their weaknesses."

Vledder snorted contemptuously.

"Gathered, no doubt, with the willing cooperation of Carla Heeten ... collected, sorted and bound by Jimmy the Blackmailer."

DeKok stared at his hands.

"There was a small fortune in secrets ... the scandal sheets would have a field day with it. From an ethical and humane point of view alone, I should have confiscated the entire collection."

"Why didn't you?"

DeKok shook his head slowly and did not answer at once. He searched his pockets until he found a piece of hard candy. He looked at it for a while, then undid the wrapper and put the candy in his mouth.

"Sometimes I still miss cigars," he said.

Vledder who had never smoked and knew for a fact that DeKok had not smoked for at least twenty years, was impatient.

"Why didn't you?" he repeated.

"What? Oh, that. No, I didn't feel like sticking my head in a hornet's nest. As long as people like Jimmy Munk and Carla Heeten are protected by the Judge-Advocate ... as long as that is allowed, I don't feel much like overstepping my authority."

Vledder was taken aback by the despondent tone in DeKok's voice.

"What are you saying?" he demanded.

DeKok sighed deeply. He looked weary and tired. Suddenly

Vledder saw him as an old man.

"Mr. Schaap, one of our own Judges-Advocate, told Carla to break her appointment with Broos."

Vledder leaned back in his chair, his mouth fell open.

"So that Dervoor could be killed quietly."

"It seems that way," said DeKok.

Vledder was baffled.

* * *

DeKok stood in front of Commissaris Buitendam's large desk. There was a determined look on his face. He realized that he had never before been in quite this situation. The thought depressed him.

"Regarding my investigation concerning the two murders in Mill's Quarter," he began in a rasping voice, "I have decided to issue no further reports."

"Why not, DeKok?" asked Buitendam. His voice was friendly.

"I have," said DeKok, "I ... for a moment I even wondered if I could trust you."

Buitendam was grave.

"That serious?"

"Yes, it is," answered DeKok. "But upon reflection I decided that, despite our differences, I have never had cause to doubt your honesty. You know I have often questioned your methods, your motives ... but *never* your honesty."

"Thank you," said Buitendam almost automatically. But it was clear that DeKok's chief was confused. "What exactly are you trying to explain, DeKok?"

"I have reasons to believe that our Judge-Advocate has illegal connections with certain underworld figures."

Buitendam was stunned.

"Mr. Schaap?"

DeKok nodded sadly.

"He deliberately kept a woman from the scene of a crime. She could have been an important witness."

Buitendam shook his head in disbelief.

"Ridiculous. Who is the witness?"

"Carla Heeten."

"The prostitute?"

The remark irritated DeKok.

"Yes," he said, clearly annoyed. "The prostitute. She told me last night that on the day of the murder of Dervoor, Mr. Schaap instructed her by phone *not* to be in her apartment between four and six in the afternoon. I would like to draw your attention to the fact that the corpse was discovered around five in the afternoon."

Commissaris Buitendam made an airy gesture.

"But DeKok," he said reasonably, "you know from experience that the statements from that ... eh, that sort of girl ... cannot always be taken seriously."

"But I *do* take them seriously," said DeKok through clenched teeth. He made every effort to control himself. "Certainly in this context. It would take too long to explain exactly why. My suspicions about Mr. Schaap are not conjured up out of thin air. From the very beginning Mr. Schaap has had a questionable role in this case."

The Commissaris could not accept that. He stood up and leaned towards DeKok.

"I forbid you to say such a thing."

DeKok sighed deeply, a martyred look on his face and in his attitude. He had known from the start that the conversation would likely degenerate in this direction. He knew his own character ... his often wild reactions to the arrogant manners of his Chief. This

162

time, too, he felt the anger boil his blood. DeKok was also aware of the near beserker rage that could grip the most placid Dutchman at times. As a rule the Dutch were some of the most tolerant and easy-going people in the world. But they could be pushed too far and then they would exhibit a behavior which was the closest thing to running amok. DeKok knew this and he controlled himself with an effort.

"Let us take the behavior of Judge-Advocate Schaap in this case point by point," he said calmly, but with a tremble in his voice.

The Commissaris was smart enough to recognize the potential for an explosion and sat down again.

"Continue," he said.

"Mr. Schaap gives me instruction to keep a watching brief at Wester Church during a baptism. Verbruggen's grandchild was to be kidnapped. Verbruggen gets additional information about the kidnapping after the baptism and discusses this with Mr. Schaap. And that same night Verbruggen is killed in an apartment in Mill's Quarter ..."

"But ..." interrupted Buitendam. DeKok held up a hand.

"There is more. When, through you, I blame Schaap for that, I am summoned to the Palace of Justice. Shortly before my arrival, Mr. Schaap has a conference that lasted about an hour with ... Jean-Paul Dervoor. A few hours later Dervoor is found dead in the same apartment. He's killed in exactly the same way as Verbruggen."

He paused to take a deep breath. It seemed to calm him some more.

"In view of all this, I find, to say the least, Mr. Schaap's behavior peculiar." He grinned without mirth. "In addition, although I clearly hinted at Schaap's recent discussion with Dervoor, he refused to make any comment about it."

Commissaris Buitendam pursed his lips and thought for a few seconds.

"I am absolutely convinced," he said eventually, "that the Judge-Advocate will be able to explain his motives to everyone's satisfaction."

DeKok sighed a tired sigh.

"Is a Judge-Advocate a Holy Man ... is he above the Law ... can a man like that not fail?"

"Not Mr. Schaap," said Buitendam with conviction.

DeKok grinned broadly. He did not feel defeated. He had saved a final trump. From the outside pocket of his jacket he produced a pistol and placed it on the desk in front of his chief.

"A particularly beautiful and expensive weapon, don't you think? Caliber 7.65 and found in the clothes of Jean-Paul Dervoor."

The Commissaris looked suspicious.

"What ... what is the matter with it?"

DeKok smiled falsely.

"Do you notice the engraved, gold initials on the grip?" He leaned forward and pointed them out. "J ... R ... S," he said to the pale face of Buitendam. "I looked it up and I found the permit for this weapon. Do you know in what name it is registered?" He paused for effect, then added quietly: "J ... R ... S ... Jules Ronald Schaap."

16

Vledder searched his partner's face.

"What did the Commissaris say?"

"I can't figure him out, especially in cases like this," shrugged DeKok. "But he seemed affected, especially when I showed him the pistol."

"Is he going to do anything?"

DeKok shook his head and sat down behind his desk.

"Not for the time being. He didn't think it was quite ethical and certainly too soon to inform the Judge-Advocate. He felt the proof was insufficient. But he *does* plan to ask for some clarification in a private conversation."

"Then what?"

"Then we'll see, as Buitendam expressed it *that the Judge-Advocate will be able to explain his motives to everyone's satisfaction.*"

"And if he can?"

"Then there's no problem," grinned DeKok. "Perhaps we'll get a better insight into the whos and wherefores of the murders and I ... I will very politely offer my apologies for a nasty, suspicious mind."

Vledder laughed.

"And if Mr. Schaap is unable to explain himself?"

DeKok looked somber.

"In that case, my boy, we'll live through some tense days."

"Why?"

"The Department of Justice doesn't like to prosecute one of its own people. Rightfully so. A failing and perhaps corrupt Mr. Schaap is no credit to the Department. We will be put under a lot of pressure to produce incontrovertible proof."

"And can we do that?"

"Perhaps," answered DeKok. "If we proceed carefully ... there are possibilities." He shook his head and there was doubt in his voice when he continued. "But in the final analysis it is not just a matter of Mr. Schaap and his more or less dubious dealings. I am much more concerned with the question as to whether or not I can ethically refuse to investigate matters for a Judge-Advocate whose character ... whose reliability is in doubt."

Vledder thought about that.

"That's a matter for your own conscience," he said carefully. "But do you really believe that Schaap has anything to do with the murders?"

DeKok nodded with conviction.

"I just don't know *where* he fits in ... what his part is in all this." He sighed. "But deep down in my heart, I hope I'm wrong."

"Why?"

"The last thing we need is negative reports in the newspapers. Police and Justice should be accepted concepts of unassailable trustworthiness." He rubbed the back of his neck. "Any news about Stella?" he asked in a different tone of voice.

Vledder shook his head as he turned to his computer. For a fleeting moment DeKok was irritated. Could Vledder not answer the simplest question without consulting his electronic memory? Then he realized that, of course, Vledder had all pertinent information in his computer and just used the machine as a check on

166

his memory. An electronic notebook, thought DeKok with approval. Once he had reduced the computer to the mechanical, non-technical aspect of a policeman's most important tool, he was satisfied in his own mind. Patiently he waited for the answers.

"I have contacted Henri LaCroix twice in the last twelve hours and there's no news. He has heard nothing. No card, no letter, no phone call and no message of any kind. No response to our APB, either. Both Stella and the Bentley have disappeared without a trace."

"Perhaps she's in the chalet in Switzerland."

"What chalet?"

"You do remember," said DeKok with a hint of sarcasm, "that Jean Baptiste Dervoor told us he used to spend his vacations in Switzerland, in the chalet owned by the Verbruggens? Also, I'm sure you remember that Verbruggen had funds available for his daughter, in Switzerland."

Vledder looked confused as he did something to his computer.

"Yes, here it is," he said. "I have the reference by young Dervoor, But that's the only entry." he looked at his mentor. "You know, Henri never once mentioned the chalet in all the discussions we've had."

"Perhaps Henri doesn't know about it. Jean Baptiste *did* speak about their youth together ... he and Stella. That was a long time before Henri appeared on the scene."

Vledder returned to his keyboard and at the same time tossed a gray folder on DeKok's desk.

"In the meantime I found Beau Robbie's real name. Little Lowee actually condescended to speak to me. He called while you were with the Chief. I pulled all relevant data. Beau Robbie is registered as Robert Arnold Beek, twenty-five, born in Amsterdam."

167

"What else?"

Vledder consulted his terminal.

"It's in the folder, there. But we don't have a record on him, that is ... as Beau Robbie. Under his real name he's listed for several assaults and a failed burglary at a jeweler's here in town."

"Weapons?"

"This is according to Lowee: Robbie was involved in an armed robbery in Arnhem. But the police there could never prove the case. There were so few clues, they didn't even bother to interrogate him."

"Connections to Jimmy Munk?" asked DeKok, studiously ignoring the folder on his desk. Vledder took it in stride.

"Little Lowee thinks that Jimmy Munk wants to hire Robbie as an enforcer."

"Oh, very nice," growled DeKok. "If you don't pay the blackmail on time, you get beat up in some dark alley."

Vledder did not comment.

"What about Robbie's connection to Carla?"

Vledder looked pensive.

"This is also from Lowee," he said. "In the underworld Carla is discussed with awe. She must be an extremely smart woman and even Jimmy doesn't have a hold on her. They say that she even feigns true, selfless love and she's good at it. She refuses payment for her ..., eh ... her services, if she thinks there will be better revenues later, through Jimmy."

DeKok grimaced.

"Women and crime ... an ideal combination, especially in connection with the Judge-Advocate." He leaned back in his chair.

Vledder waited. He knew the signs.

DeKok leaned back and stared at the ceiling. It was as if a light had suddenly come on. He saw a thread, the glimmer of an idea. It was still vague, but the larger outlines of the structure were almost recognizable. Suddenly he stood up and stepped to the peg to get his coat.

Vledder came to his feet at the same time.

"Where are we going?"

"To Dovecote." said DeKok.

"Why?" asked Vledder as he followed his partner out of the room.

"I want to ask Mrs. Kolfs a few more questions." He smiled faintly. "And I want to ask her if *she* knows Pete."

* * *

The yellow narcissus were still in bloom. DeKok passed by without paying attention. With Vledder he approached the door of 765 and pushed the bell. A few moments later a voice came from the small loudspeaker.

"Who is there?"

They recognized Mrs. Kolfs' voice.

"Inspector DeKok," he said. "You may remember us, from Warmoes Street station. My colleague and I would like to talk to you."

"One moment," answered the speaker.

In less than a minute the door was opened. Mrs Kolfs held open the door. A happy smile of recognition lit up her face. She wore the same dark slacks and black sweater as during their fist visit. Again DeKok was attracted by her ripe, statuesque beauty. A bit stiff, his hat over his heart, he bowed.

"I'm sorry," he said, "that we have to bother you once again." He shrugged an apology. "But it is inevitable in our profession. There are always more questions and always more things that need to be explained."

"Not at all, please come in, gentlemen."

She led the way to the living room. Surreptitiously DeKok glanced carefully around the room. Nothing seemed to have changed from their last visit. But this time the green, velvet curtains were thrown open and cheerful sunlight came through the windows and played with a crystal carafe on the table.

After Mrs. Kolfs had seated herself, DeKok looked around openly.

"Is Marius not here?"

She shook her head, smiling.

"Marius went to a meeting."

DeKok nodded his understanding.

"Did you know that Marius created a scene at his father's funeral?"

"I heard that," she answered. "Marius should not have done that, I spoke to him about it. One should respect death as it is strictly impartial."

"Death?"

"Yes ...death. When it calls there is no escape."

DeKok gave her a searching look.

"Are you familiar with the following text: *I have called thee by thy name; thou art Mine*?"

A new smile appeared on her face.

"That is not a call to Death ... but a call for Life. Our Dear Lord calls you by name in order to belong to Him. You understand ... that is why the text is often used during a baptism."

DeKok looked at her serene face.

"It was the text for your grandchild's baptism."

"I was not invited."

"Have you ever seen your grandchild?"

She shook her head.

"My husband always prevented that. When I finally con-

170

fronted him with it, he said that the child was named after *him* and that Stella's child could never be *my* grandchild."

DeKok cocked his head at her and listened carefully to the undertones in her voice.

"How much of the hate against your husband have you instilled in Marius?"

She looked shocked.

"Marius is old and wise enough," she said crisply, "to develop his own feelings of love and hate."

"Was he old and wise enough seven years ago, when you divorced?"

There was an alert look in her eyes.

"What are you driving at, Inspector?"

"I'm merely looking for a motive for the murder of your husband, your ex-husband. Perhaps you have heard that Jean-Paul Dervoor has also been killed."

She gave him a sad smile.

"I'm not surprised."

"You expected it?"

"More or less."

"Why?"

"Jean-Paul Dervoor was just as corrupt as my husband."

DeKok was amused.

"Death is not always impartial. I know a lot of corrupt people who live merrily on."

The remark seemed to offend Mrs. Kolfs. She rose from her chair. There was something demonstrative about the movement ... as if announcing the end of the interview.

With a sigh DeKok picked up his hat from the floor.

"Have you any idea who could have killed these men?"

"No." she said. Her voice was like ice.

DeKok stood up. Despite her attitude, a friendly smile remained on his face.

"Do you know a certain Pete?"

Mrs. Kolfs wilted momentarily.

"What's the matter with Pete?"

"You know him?"

"Yes."

"Long?"

"We were friends."

"When?"

She bit her lower lip and suddenly there was a small, lace handkerchief in her hands.

"Before I met my husband, Pete and I loved each other. Until he met a young woman. He loved her even more and they decided to live together. Officially they never married."

"Were you hurt by this?"

Mrs. Kolfs did not answer and DeKok did not insist.

"Do you know Pete's whereabouts?"

She shook her head. Her eyes were damp with the beginning of tears.

"I haven't heard from him for years."

DeKok leaned closer.

"Why did Pete want your husband dead?"

17

Mrs. Kolfs paled. Her lower lip trembled and tiredly she fell back in the chair.

"Albert ... Albert Verbruggen sent Pete to jail."

"Jail?"

Mrs. Kolfs closed her eyes.

"My husband said that Pete had committed fraud and the bank had lost tens of thousands because of it."

"The Ysselstein Bank?" asked DeKok.

She nodded without opening her eyes.

"I never wanted to believe it," she said. "One day my husband told me that my so-called boyfriend, that's what he called Pete, was a crook and a thief. When I argued that with him, he showed me documents that Pete was supposed to have signed. There were forged property deeds on the basis of which Pete had borrowed from the bank." She paused, lost in memory. "I begged my husband to handle the matter quietly, to keep the Police out of it. But he laughed at me and told me that I should have been more careful about picking my friends."

"Not very nice."

She shook her head and opened her eyes.

"Albert was not very nice."

"But why would your husband want to accuse Pete of fraud?

I don't understand that. It makes no sense." He looked at her earnestly. "Did your ... did your affection for Pete have anything to do with it?"

Mrs. Kolfs shrugged and blew her nose.

"I had told my husband about Pete. Why not? There was nothing left between us. We were just distant friends. As soon as Pete moved in with his woman, his common-law wife actually, he had hardly any time left for me. I suffered because of that, there's no denying it. But I understood that someone new had come into his life. After that I may have met him just once, or twice. And that was always just coincidence. Nothing planned, I mean."

"So your husband had no reason to be jealous?"

"Certainly not. I have *never* given him the least cause to be jealous." A bitter smile played around her lips. "But Albert regularly visited prostitutes within six months after we were married."

DeKok did not pursue that subject.

"And despite your pleading, your husband notified the Police?"

"Yes."

"When was that?"

"About seven years ago."

DeKok looked thoughtful.

"Did your divorce have anything to do with Pete?"

She did not answer, but bowed her head. It was as if she sank back in memories. Silently she tore at the lace handkerchief in her hands. DeKok insisted.

"Did your divorce have anything to do with Pete?" he repeated.

She looked up with vague eyes. Then she nodded.

"It contributed to the divorce, yes, that's the word. It was a contributory factor. As long as strangers were the victims of my husband's manipulations, it was bearable, barely ... but bearable.

I was upset, but in a real sense it did not touch me. Only after my husband had connived to send Pete to jail, although he was innocent. Only then did I realize how much grief and sorrow my husband had caused people."

DeKok rubbed his chin.

"Did Marius know about Pete?"

"Yes."

"And?"

"Marius despised his father. That is why he rejected any inheritance."

DeKok nodded thoughtfully and looked at Vledder. Vledder was busy making notes and did not look up.

"How many years did Pete get?" asked DeKok.

Mrs. Kolfs made a helpless gesture.

"I don't know. With that and the distress of the divorce, it escaped me."

The gray sleuth remained pensive.

"Which Judge-Advocate," he asked suddenly, "handled the prosecution?"

Mrs. Kolfs placed her hands in her lap. There was a resigned attitude in her body, but there was a malicious fire in her eyes.

"Jules ... Jules Schaap."

* * *

"Peter Bower."

DeKok nodded with emphasis.

"That's the one ... the man, who spoke the deadly threats to Blonde Hennie and young Dervoor."

Vledder moved around in his chair until he was comfortable. "The killer?"

DeKok did not answer at once. For a long time he stared into the distance. There was a serious expression on his face. The latest information had set his thoughts adrift and he suddenly realized that the investigation had reached a decisive stage.

"Peter Bower," he said carefully. "Fits exactly into the picture of the murderer, as I visualize it. A man with a passion, an inner drive, driven by an implacable hatred. When Mrs. Kolfs told us that Peter and Dervoor were students together, that they had both studied engineering at the University in Delft ... I was almost convinced."

"Almost?" wondered Vledder. "It *has* to be him. It's almost impossible for it to be anyone else. You said it yourself. He was the man who uttered the deadly threats. He knew both men ... and he had a motive."

DeKok waved a finger at his young partner.

"Only in reference to Verbruggen."

"What do you mean?"

"According to Mrs. Kolfs, it was her ex-husband, Verbruggen, who fabricated the false evidence that sent Bower to jail. That does not give us a motive for the killing of Dervoor."

"There was some connection," exclaimed Vledder, slamming a fist on the arm of his chair. "And it must have been a close connection, some sort of relationship. Dervoor called him 'Pete' and that proves it." Sometimes Vledder was carried away by enthusiasm for his own theories.

DeKok grinned.

"Perhaps, but then Dervoor was also the one who said that 'Pete' wouldn't have the nerve to kill."

Vledder stood up. His face was red.

"That was seven years ago. He had not been in jail. Maybe he found the nerve."

DeKok smiled smugly. He liked Vledder's enthusiastic outbursts.

"Perhaps," he said soothingly, "we should gather some extensive information about Bower. As of now we only have his name." He pointed at Vledder's computer. "Can you do anything with your box of tricks? You asked both Hennie and Jean Baptiste to go through our Picture Gallery, didn't you?"

"Yes."

"And the man we're looking for was not in our records, according to them?"

Vledder slapped his forehead.

"You're right! If Peter Bower has a jail record, he *must* be in our collection."

DeKok nodded.

"It's possible, of course, that he has changed so much that neither Blonde Hennie, nor young Dervoor, could recognize him from the files." He made a gesture of dismissal. "But we can worry about that later. We can always confront them in person ... when the time comes. But our priority is to find him as soon as possible ... before there is a third victim."

"What!?" exclaimed Vledder. "A *third* victim? Who?"

"Jules Ronald Schaap," sighed DeKok. "You see what you can find out while I see Buitendam. He wants to talk to me."

"Keep your cool," admonished Vledder.

DeKok did not dignify that with an answer.

* * *

Commissaris Buitendam waved with an elegant hand.

"This time I really would appreciate it, if you sat down, De-Kok." His voice was solemn, but with a friendly undertone. He waited until DeKok had grudgingly pulled up a chair. "This morning I had a long conversation with the Judge-Advocate ... as promised." He hesitated for a moment. "Mr. Schaap impressed me as being rather defeated or discomfitted. Especially after I explained your view of the matter ... your ...eh, your accusations. And I must tell you honestly that I was not impressed with Mr. Schaap's degree of forthrightness. He told me he needed time to consider ... that he would announce his definitive point of view at a later point in time. Until then he's giving you carte blanche."

DeKok sat up straight. The first part of Buitendam's speech he had barely heard. The usual whitewash, he thought. But the last words made him sit up. He looked at his Chief with incredulity.

"Carte blanche?"

Commissaris Buitendam nodded emphatically.

"You can conduct your investigation completely free of any interference ... even if certain facts were to become apparent that may incriminate the Judge-Advocate."

"And that is likely to happen?"

Buitendam was obviously displeased.

"You will understand that I did not raise *that* question. I found it irrelevant within the scope of our conversation. But ... in view of his attitude in regard to the revelations so far, we must assume that such a development is within the realm of possibilities."

He could have just said 'yes,' thought DeKok, but did not voice it.

"Why doesn't he tell me everything I need to know? Surely that would be best for all parties concerned."

Buitendam shrugged.

"I believe he wants to reflect on his own position first."

"Did Mr. Schaap instruct Carla *not* to go to her apartment? Did he give Jean-Paul Dervoor his pistol? Does he know the killer?"

"I am sorry, DeKok. I cannot give you an answer to any of

these questions. I did not implicitly ask them. It is my considered opinion, however, that Mr. Schaap is very much entangled in this affair. Your insight, your instincts, are correct." The Commissaris smiled thinly. "You will not be surprised, I'm certain," he added.

DeKok ignored the implied praise.

"What exactly does *carte blanche* mean?"

Commissaris Buitendam rummaged among the papers on his desk.

"I have here," he announced, "a declaration, signed by Mr. Schaap, to the effect that everything you do in this case has his personal, prior approval."

DeKok snorted, but was nevertheless impressed.

"Pretty sweeping," he commented.

Buitendam handed him the paper.

"I hope, DeKok, that you will use it with discretion."

DeKok stood up. Triumph sang in his heart and he suppressed the urge to depart with a mocking comment. But he could be magnanimous in victory.

"Thank you," said DeKok humbly. "I'll try."

He looked back when he reached the door. The expression on Buitendam's face was hard to read, but suddenly, for no apparent reason, DeKok felt pity for his Chief.

* * *

Elated, DeKok walked into the large, busy detective room. His legs and calves seemed to have been rejuvenated. With a spring in his step he approached Vledder's desk.

"Come, my boy," he cried out jovially, "let's hit the road. Mr. Schaap has changed his tack. He has more or less admitted that he's involved in the case." He waved the piece off paper under Vledder's nose. "We have carte blanche and nothing can stand in our way. We can pick up Peter Bower anytime. How far have you got. Do you have an address, a town ..." He stopped suddenly when he saw Vledder's face. "Something the matter?" he asked, uncertain about how to interpret the look on Vledder's face.

Vledder dropped his head. With the back of one hand he rubbed dry lips.

"There is nothing left to find."

"What *do* you mean?"

The young Inspector looked pale and confused.

"Peter Bower ... Peter Bower is dead."

DeKok sat down on the edge of Vledder's desk.

"Dead ... when ... how?"

Vledder swallowed.

"He died almost four months ago from an ongoing illness ... in the prison hospital in Scheveningen."*

---

* Upon their death, all records (photo's, fingerprints, etc.) of suspects and inmates are removed from Police Registers.

18

DeKok fell down in his chair behind the desk. He looked tired. The news that Peter Bower had died four months ago had shocked him. Again an entire theory collapsed.

He rubbed his flat hands over his face. From between spread fingers he looked at Vledder at the desk next to him. The young Inspector also looked defeated. Less than half an hour ago both had been jubilant that the solution to the puzzle was near at hand and that the arrest of the killer would merely be a matter of time. Now it seemed that they were as far removed from a solution as that sunny Sunday morning in Wester Church.

The gray sleuth stood up and began to pace through the room. He tried to bring some sort of order to his chaotic thoughts.

Vledder played with his keyboard. It was his way of doodling. Both men were deep in thought.

Peter Bower, reflected DeKok, had to play an important role in the overall situation. Perhaps the conclusion was not rational, but in this case he knew that his instincts were correct. Peter Bower was a key figure in the affair.

Seven years ago the man declared that he was after the lives of Verbruggen and Dervoor. Why? If Mrs. Kolfs was right, and he had every reason to believe that this was so, why did Verbruggen forge documents that sent Peter Bower to jail? What was the background to that? Did Mr. Schaap, as prosecutor, know the evidence was forged? If so, why did he not speak out? Why did he use his position to help condemn Peter Bower? Were Carla Heeten and Jimmy Munk aware of the backgrounds of this dark game? Was there a folder marked 'Peter Bower' in the safe at Seadike?"

DeKok pressed both hands against his ears. The questions seemed to thunder in his head. And the same question overwhelming all the others, was louder the more he tried to ignore it: If Peter Bower did not commit the murders ... then who?

He stopped in front of Vledder's desk.

"How much did Peter Bower get for that alleged fraud?"

"Two and a half years, thirty months."

DeKok whistled softly.

"Pretty stiff for fraud."

"It is."

Then DeKok looked puzzled.

"He died in prison four months ago?"

Vledder nodded and looked at his terminal.

"Yes, his time was not up. He had at least three months left to go before his release."

DeKok rubbed the bridge of his nose with a little finger.

"When was the conviction?"

"About seven years ago," answered Vledder. "At about the time he made the threats to Hennie and Jean Baptiste Dervoor. But it was a verdict in absentia. The day before the trial he left for France."

"Request for deportation?"

"No. About three years ago he returned to Holland of his own free will. He walked around as a free man for some time, but was eventually arrested to begin his sentence."

DeKok nodded his understanding. He pulled out his lower

lip and let it plop back. He repeated the annoying gesture several times. For a moment he looked indecisive. Then he walked with quick steps to the peg to get his hat and coat. Vledder followed.

"Where are we going?" asked Vledder.

"Princes Canal ... Palace of Justice. I want to see the Court file on Peter Bower ... including the final verdict and the transcript of the case." His face was expressionless. "And," DeKok continued, "I'll raise hell if the file happens to have disappeared."

The phone rang on DeKok's desk. Vledder looked at his partner.

"Shall I answer it?"

DeKok nodded.

"You never know. Perhaps it's the killer who wants to give himself up."

Vledder laughed briefly and walked back to pick up the receiver. DeKok watched from a distance. Vledder's face became serious as he listened. After a while he replaced the receiver.

"That was Mr. Schaap," he said as he rejoined DeKok.

"*Our* Mr. Schaap?"

Vledder nodded.

"He has received a threatening letter. He's expected in Carla's apartment at eight o'clock tonight."

* * *

The sharp gaze of DeKok roamed around the room. He carefully took in everything he saw. The imposing seating arrangement in cream colored leather ... the soft pink wall hangings ... the stylish whatnot and the sad Pierrot in white ceramic.

He rubbed the back of his neck. He wrestled with a strange sense of confusion. Although he was convinced he was right, he could not rid himself of a feeling of uncertainty. He sighed deeply and banished the thoughts of failure to the back of his mind.

The gray sleuth looked at Vledder and Raap, who had been pressed into service for this particular operation. With arms folded across their chests, they leaned against a wall. Their faces were somber, aware of the seriousness of the situation.

"We must make sure we take every possible precaution," began DeKok. He looked at his watch. "We have almost an hour before the murderer arrives. The trouble is that we cannot offer Mr. Schaap much in the way of protection. If the killer is not absolutely convinced he's alone with his victim, he may not go through with it. Therefore we *must* remain invisible ... until he has provided enough evidence that can lead to a conviction." He turned toward Schaap. "You don't have to worry that the killer will start shooting at once. He will take his time. First he will tell you why he has decided to kill you. As long as you're standing, you'll not be in danger. The danger will be when you're on your knees."

Schaap swallowed.

"How ... how do you mean?"

DeKok looked at him coldly.

"Exactly as I said. The killer will want to humiliate you first. He will want you to go down on your knees and beg for mercy."

Schaap coughed, trying to regain some semblance of authority.

"How do you know that?" he asked sharply.

DeKok grinned a crooked smile.

"If you had taken the trouble to read our reports carefully ... and if you had been able to make the connection ... then you would have known as well. Both victims, Verbruggen and Dervoor had fiber traces of the carpet on the knees of their trousers. Fibers from *this* ..." he tapped the floor with a foot, "white woolen carpet. You understand now, Mr. Schaap? Both men went beg-

184

ging to their death. They were begging for their life and, perhaps, for forgivenes." He tapped the Judge-Advocate lightly on the chest. "And," he added, "the killer has planned the same sort of death for you."

Suddenly Schaap looked pale. He had lost the last vestige of bluster. His mouth was half open and his hands shook.

"When ... when will you intervene?" he asked with a trembling voice.

DeKok smiled.

"As I said, as soon as I think we have enough evidence. You must know from experience how careful our Courts are before they pass a guilty verdict."

It sounded sarcastic and was meant to be. DeKok took another close look at the man who had probably been responsible for the conviction of at least one innocent man. There was cold fear in the eyes of Mr. Schaap. Sweat stood out on his upper lip. With a sudden change of mood, DeKok was quickly overcome with pity for the frightened official. He leaned closer.

"You can still withdraw," suggested DeKok.

Mr. Schaap hesitated for a few seconds. Then he shook his head, a new look of determination on his face.

"No, DeKok," he said with a quiver in his voice. "I will not withdraw, nor will I hide. Not now, not ever again."

The gray sleuth placed an encouraging hand on the other's shoulder.

"I wish you strength," DeKok said simply. It sounded like a prayer.

* * *

DeKok looked at his watch. It was seven minutes to eight. They had been in their more or less strategic positions for about fifteen minutes. The murderer should be surprised when he least expected it. And, if at all possible, in a compromising position. There must be no ambiguities, no doubts, no question marks. DeKok did not want to give any lawyer, no matter how clever, the opportunity to finagle a non-guilty verdict, to circumvent justice. From the spot where he had concealed himself he had a reasonably good view of the room ... the cream colored couch and the pink, standing lamp. He had been careful not to make any changes in the decor, even if that would have meant a better view. The murderer, he realized, was too familiar with the decor of the room. Any deviation would be immediately spotted and might result in a change of plans. Through the frosted glass room divider he was able to make out the silhouette of the Judge-Advocate. The man paced nervously up and down.

DeKok suddenly remembered that he had not checked underneath the Pierrot to see whether or not there was a message there. He hoped fervently that the killer would bring it with him. It would be additional evidence.

A little distance away, near the door of the bedroom, he heard Vledder's quiet breathing. The sound was familiar. For a fleeting moment DeKok thought about their joint battles against crime. Not counting the small skirmishes, this was at least the seventeenth, or eighteenth major case Vledder and he had worked together. By now he knew the temper of his young partner's character ... his strengths and weaknesses. He had impressed on Vledder to control his emotions and to wait for the right moment.

Again DeKok glanced at his watch. Time went by slowly. It was just a few minutes past eight.

Suddenly he heard the clicking of the latch on the front door. He tensed. The front door slammed shut. There was the sound of footsteps in the foyer. Then, abruptly there was a second silhouette. Slowly it approached the silhouette of Mr. Schaap. There

186

was the sound of voices ... vague noises ... words which could not be understood.

DeKok watched the two silhouettes close together. Despite the lack of detail, it seemed that Mr. Schaap's silhouette expressed surprise and fear. There was some sort of dialog ... calm, without the rasing of voices.

Suddenly, there was the decisive moment. Mr. Schaap's silhouette seemed to shrink. His hands reached out, came together, as if in prayer.

DeKok yelled out and suddenly there was a lot of noise ... the rush of footsteps and the short, barking sounds of gun shots. When DeKok reached the living room, Mr. Schaap lay bleeding on the carpet. Frans Raap leaned over the assailant and Vledder knelt down next to Mr. Schaap. Raap disarmed the killer and roughly pulled the man by his collar to a standing position. Vledder looked up.

"Henri LaCroix," panted Vledder.

19

The doorbell rang and Mrs. DeKok opened the door.

"Celine," she cried out, "how lovely to see you."

Vledder and his fiance, Celine stood on the doorstep. Celine was a flight attendant for KLM, Royal Dutch Airlines, and did not spend much time in Holland. Mrs. DeKok who looked upon Vledder as a son, thoroughly approved of Celine.

Vledder grinned in the background as the two women embraced. Then he produced a large bouquet of roses and offered them to his partner's wife. She thanked him.

"Go into the living room," she urged. "Frans Raap is already here. I'll just put these in a vase."

As Vledder opened the door of the living room, DeKok jumped up in delighted surprise.

"Celine," he said, "how wonderful you happen to be in town."

"We cannot stay long," apologized Vledder. "We're on the way to the airport. Celine has a night flight out."

DeKok looked benignly at his partner and his beautiful fiance. Celine was almost as tall as Vledder and just as blonde. A slender figure and long legs were emphasized by the trim KLM uniform. Frans Raap also stood up and was now introduced.

"Please, sit down," invited DeKok.

Mrs. DeKok came in, carrying a vase with the roses displayed to perfection. She placed the vase on a sideboard and addressed her husband.

"Go ahead, Jurriaan, pour. I'll be right back."

DeKok had produced an extra glass for Celine and started to pour a very fine cognac into the waiting snifters.

"Not for me," said Celine. "I'm flying."

"Oh, of course," said DeKok. "Can we get you something else?"

Mrs. DeKok reentered the room with a large tray of assorted delicacies. On one side of the tray was a glass and a bottle of ginger ale. She placed the tray on the table and handed Celine the ginger ale.

"We see too little of you," she said. "But I haven't forgotten."

"Thank you," said Celine, "I feel like an intruder."

"Nonsense," blustered DeKok. "you're always welcome. A sight for sore eyes," he joked as he handed the filled snifters around to the others.

"To crime," said Vledder, as they raised their glasses.

For several minutes they silently enjoyed the excellent liquor, while Celine sipped her ginger ale. Over the rim of her glass she studied the others. How strangely relaxed they looked, she thought. She knew of the tensions of their daily work and wondered where they found the strength. DeKok caught her glance and smiled at her.

"How is Mr. Schaap doing," asked Mrs. DeKok.

"Reasonable, reasonable," said DeKok. "He's home again. The bullets did relatively little damage, no vital parts were hit. Flesh wounds, really."

Vledder leaned forward.

"But in the papers it was reported that he had been fatally

shot."

"A small ruse on my part," twinkled DeKok. "At my express request, the papers have not been told the full story. You probably also noticed that Henri's arrest has not been mentioned, either."

"Why?" asked Celine who had only a sketchy knowledge of what had gone on before. She had been out of the country for most of it and Vledder hardly ever discussed his work when they finally managed to spend some time together.

DeKok winked at her, but did not answer the question. From his pocket he produced a small object. It was wafer thin, one inch wide and about two inches long. With the small protrusions on the side, it resembled a flat centipede.

"Extremely compact miniaturization," he said. "A miniaturization of complicated switching capabilities, specifically designed to connect an almost unlimited number of computers together in any desired combination." He grinned. "In other words ... a super chip."

Vledder gaped at him. His partner, who detested most forms of modern technology, who refused to carry a cell phone, or a walkie-talkie and who referred to his computer as a wonder box. He, who had never even switched on the computer on his desk at the station, was now using words as if he knew what he was talking about.

DeKok noticed Vledder's look.

"Don't worry," he said, as he handed the small object around for the others to study. "I've not taken leave of my senses, but in order to know what was going on, I had to learn the jargon. Anyway," he confessed, "Jean Baptiste Dervoor told me what to say."

He took a sip from his glass.

"Speaking of Jean Baptiste, he supplied me with this sample from the inventory at Electronics International."

Mrs. DeKok gave her husband a strange look.

"What's the purpose of all this, I thought you would tell us about the murders."

DeKok reached over and squeezed her hand affectionately.

"I was just getting to that," he assured her. "This particular super-chip is the invention of a man whose life undeservedly ended in jail."

"Peter Bower," guessed Raap.

"Exactly, Peter Bower, an extremely gifted man, who all by himself and without the benefit of a laboratory, invented this super-chip ... an invention that should have been the crowning glory of his ingenuity, but instead led to abject humiliation."

He paused and took back the sample and placed it in a box.

"The management of Electronics International," continued DeKok, "a Dutch company with connections worldwide, realized that they could obtain a nearly untouchable monopoly, if they could produce the chip in quantity. When rumors of the invention reached Jean-Paul Dervoor, he contacted Peter Bower, whom he had known as a student. Jean-Paul tried to make Peter an offer he couldn't refuse."

Mrs. DeKok looked at her husband.

"But he refused anyway," she said.

"Yes, Peter Bower was of the opinion that the world wasn't ready for his invention. He thought it was too soon and wanted to delay circulation."

"Then what happened?" asked Celine when DeKok stopped to refill his glass. Raap held out his glass to be refilled, as well. Vledder refused a second glass.

"One is enough, thank you. I still have to drive."

"Why don't you take a cab?" asked Raap.

"No, Celine will drive to the airport and by then it should be safe enough for me to drive back."

"Then I'll get some coffee now," said Mrs. DeKok. She

turned to her husband.

"Go ahead and answer Celine's question," she said. "I'll catch up."

"Very well. One night armed burglars entered Peter Bower's house and stole everything connected with the super-chip ... designs, drawings, models, computer disks, the works. Peter suspected that the burglary was instigated by Jean-Paul Dervoor, who had used his firm's money to hire the necessary muscle. Although he could never prove it, he held the company responsible and threatened them with exposure, if they ever produced and sold the chip."

Vledder grinned.

"Electronics International had the invention, but could not exploit it."

DeKok nodded.

"Jean-Paul Dervoor discussed the matter with his banker, Albert Verbruggen. While he was developing his idea, Peter Bower had borrowed small sums from the Ysselstein bank. Verbruggen thought he had a way to remove the bothersome and threatening presence of Bower. He changed some of the paperwork Bower had offered as security for the loans and with those he went to his friend Schaap and accused Bower of fraud."

DeKok paused. Mrs DeKok returned in the room with a tray laden with a coffeepot, cream, sugar and cups and saucers. Celine hastened to help her. Vledder and Celine both took coffee. The others helped themselves to the delicacies prepared earlier. Mrs. DeKok sat down next to her husband.

"Go on," she urged.

"Whether or not Mr. Schaap saw through the falsifications, I do not know, Perhaps he just accepted at face value the evidence provided by his friend Verbruggen. Whatever ... the Judge-Advocate decided on prosecution. And that ... was the prelude to the recent murders."

"To be honest, I don't quite see the connection," ventured Fans Raap.

"Understandable," said DeKok. "You've only been marginally involved in the case. What happened is, that Peter Bower did not go to jail ... that is, not immediately. Before the trial he fled to France. He would have liked to take his wife, his common-law wife, with him, but she was not well and he did not think she would survive the life of a fugitive. Three years ago her condition worsened enough to lure Bower back from his self-imposed exile. They were together for another two months. Then Maria LaCroix died."

"Maria LaCroix?" asked Vledder. The revelation was a surprise to him as well.

"Henri's mother," confessed DeKok.

"So, Peter Bower is ..."

"... the biological father of Henri LaCroix," completed De-Kok. "Maria and Peter were not legally married, remember? So naturally any offspring would get the last name of the mother."

"It's becoming clear," said Mrs. DeKok. The others nodded their agreement.

"Of course," said Vledder, "it was ..."

DeKok held up a hand to interrupt.

"It was not until he attended his father's last hours in the prison hospital, that Henri put the whole thing together, became fully aware of what had happened. Young LaCroix was upset. embittered, that his father and mother had been hurt and humiliated to such an extent. He realized that three people had been instrumental in ruining his parents' lives and he swore that he would personally see to it that they were avenged. At the time Henri really meant that, he told me. By the time he drove home, after his father had passed away, he realized that such vengeance would not right the wrongs."

DeKok drained his glass and reached for the bottle.

"No, you don't," warned his wife. Celine and Dick have to leave soon and you're going to finish this first."

DeKok grinned ruefully and leaned back in his chair.

"There's not much left to tell. When Henri came home he told his wife about his father's death ... the sad story of his life and the promise he had made himself. Much to his surprise, Stella immediately agreed with him. She pressed Henri in keeping the promise he had made at his father's deathbed. And it was *her* suggestion that the first victim would be Verbruggen."

"Her own father?" Mrs, DeKok was shocked.

"Yes. Her own father. Once Henri agreed, she pushed him to continue. It was her plan to have the killings take place in Carla's apartment. She knew that Jimmy Munk had been blackmailing her father and his friends for years and she figured it would steer the Police in the wrong direction."

"But why?" asked Celine, who heard everything for the first time. Unlike Vledder and Raap, she had no prior knowledge of any of the details. Even Mrs. DeKok knew bits and pieces.

DeKok made a helpless gesture.

"In almost every investigation I have made mistakes. Some small and some really important ones. I've always been upset about that and I try not to repeat any mistakes I may have made. But I have also learned that mistakes are almost inevitable. Our work is designed for mistakes. I knew about a woman who could have helped me to avoid a number of errors in this case ... if I had taken the trouble to call on her, talk with her. But for one reason, or another, I kept putting it off. Something else always seemed more important."

Vledder frowned.

"Who are you talking about?"

"Verbruggen's housekeeper in Laren. But as soon as I had heard Henri's story, I *did* contact her. She told me that Stella had an affair of long standing with some television director. Laren is close to Hilversum, you know."

Mrs. DeKok nodded. Like everyone else, she knew that Hilversum was the broadcast center of the Netherlands. Holland is too small to need regional transmitters and does not have regional stations as a result. All radio and television broadcasts originate from once central point. The various broadcast companies share studio and technical facilities. The antennas can be seen for miles around.

"Yes, we know, oh procrastinating husband," mocked Mrs. DeKok.

"Very well," said DeKok, "the rest is easily explained. According to the housekeeper, the child that was baptized a few weeks ago, is probably not Henri's child. The housekeeper also agreed with the assessment of Stella's mother. Both women think that Stella and her father have a lot of undesirable qualities in common. Both are hard, pitiless and without mercy. When Stella heard that Marius had rejected his inheritance, she must have concocted a plan to get her father's money as soon as possible, even if she had to kill him."

"Henri's promise must have been like music to her ears," commented Frans Raap.

"What Stella wants Stella gets," sang Vledder in an awful voice.

"Eh, what?" asked DeKok.

"I was reminded," said Vledder, of what Jean Baptiste Dervoor said about Stella at one time. He said: *If Stella wanted something it just happened* ... and that reminded me of a song *What Lola wants, Lola gets*. That's all."

"Oh, yes," said Mrs. DeKok. "A musical called `Damn Yankees.' Lola was a devil, wasn't she?"

"What Yankees," questioned DeKok. "Never heard of it."

"Of course not, love," said his wife, "you would probably have called it *Darn* Yankees."

They all laughed. DeKok looked sheepish.

"We have to go," announced Vledder.

Frans Raap also decided to leave. He did not want to overstay his welcome and although both DeKok and his wife assured him that was impossible, Frans insisted on calling a taxi.

"Have a good trip," DeKok wished Celine. Mrs. DeKok gave her a big hug and wished her the same. Vledder waved and, accompanied by Raap, the guests left.

* * *

Mrs. DeKok came back in the living room and started to clear away the remains of the party. DeKok stood up to help.

"No, no," said Mrs. DeKok. "Sit down and have another drink. I'll just make some fresh coffee."

After a while she returned with a fresh pot of coffee and poured for them both. Then she sat down next to her husband and took one of his hands in both of hers.

"All *my* questions have not been answered," she said, shaking her head. "While your colleagues were here, I did not want to say anything ... besides Vledder and Celine had to leave. But how is it possible that two such intelligent people as Verbruggen and Dervoor were so easily led into a trap?"

DeKok gave her a fond smile.

"Money," he said. "Money is power. And power is the highest form of right. There is a famous saying that gives a perfect example of that: *hoc volo, sic jubeo, sit pro ratione voluntas.* Or, freely translated: *This is what I want, that is what I order and my*

197

desire is sufficient reason. This sort of arrogant opinion is found among many rich and influential people. In their pride they think they can tackle any obstacle ... overcome any problem."

Mrs. DeKok seemed annoyed.

"Perhaps that explains why it took you so long to find the facts, but I want to know why they went to that apartment. What was in the letters? What made them go?"

"I never read the letters that induced them to go," he said slowly. "But Henri LaCroix told me the gist of the letters. The one addressed to Verbruggen read, in part: *If you want to know more about the kidnapping, come to Carla's apartment.* After the killing, Henri removed the letter from the corpse, because he felt he had made a big mistake."

"Mistake?"

"Yes, The two letters Verbruggen showed me, had been mailed. But the letter that Henri used to entice his father-in-law to the apartment, was already in Henri's pocket during the church service. He managed to pass the letter to Verbruggen when they arrived in Laren. This letter had *not* come through the mail. That was impossible, because the post office does not deliver on Sunday. He told Verbruggen it was found among some unopened mail from the Saturday delivery, but he realized that the Police would want to know more when they noticed the letter had not gone through the postal system. Verbruggen himself was too upset to notice and actually told Mr. Schaap the same story, about finding it in Saturday's mail."

"Then why was Henri worried?"

"Because he did not know what Verbruggen had told Schaap and because, as I said, the Police would immediately notice the absence of a stamp, or cancellation on the envelope. Both envelope and letter had to disappear. Dervoor was even easier. That letter was mailed and it said, in part: *I posses all specifications for the super-chip you stole. You can hear my terms at 5 o'clock in Carla's apartment. Otherwise I'll sell it to Japan.* Dervoor went into a panic. It was not just himself who was threatened, but also his company. In addition Henri signed the letter with the name Peter Bower."

"What?"

DeKok grinned.

"I could not have been clearer."

"But Peter Bower was already dead."

"Of course. And both Dervoor and Schaap knew it. That is what terrified them so. They could no longer even guess from where the danger was coming. In any case, they were certain that, in contrast with Bower, they were dealing with a man who had indeed the audacity and willingness to kill. Verbruggen's death could have been explained a number of ways, but after the second letter, Schaap and Dervoor realized that the banker had fallen victim to a heretofore completely unknown threat."

Mrs. DeKok shook her head in wonder.

"And yet Dervoor went to the apartment."

"He had no choice. He and Schaap discussed the best course of action to take. If they informed me, they knew that the Bower situation would also surface. Something they wanted to avoid at all cost."

"I can see that."

"Anyway, Dervoor thought he could come to an agreement. After all, if it was a matter of money ... he could dispose of vast sums. Just to be on the safe side, Schaap lent him his pistol. Armed and laboring under a misapprehension about the extent of the problem, Dervoor met his end."

It sounded cynical.

"What was in Schaap's letter?"

"That too, was almost irresistible. It said, in part: *If you want to know why Dervoor and Verbruggen died, then come ...*"

Mrs. DeKok nodded sadly.

"And then Mr. Schaap was finally persuaded to put all his cards on the table and informed you."

"Exactly."

"What about Jimmy Munk?"

"On my advice, Mr. Schaap has informed the Judge-Advocate in Seadike. That safe was opened yesterday and earlier tonight Jimmy and Carla were arrested in a Rotterdam hotel. They're still looking for Robbie."

"And Stella?"

The gray sleuth smiled thinly.

"Earlier Vledder asked me why the reports in the papers were in error. They were deliberately misleading. Dutch newspapers are also read in other countries, such as Switzerland. I had a strong suspicion that Stella was hiding out in Switzerland, but really almost any country in Europe would have done as well. Sooner or later a Dutchman will pick up a Dutch paper and Stella was more than any other likely to do so. She would want to be kept informed."

He sipped his coffee and poured himself and his wife another cup. He settled back in his chair.

"As it happens," he picked up the narrative, "Henri LaCroix later confirmed that Stella was in Switzerland all along. Despite his denials, he was in regular contact with his wife. Because of my ... eh, my misinformation, Stella thinks that Henri has completed his vengeance ... and is still at large."

With a tired gesture he reached into the breast pocket of his shirt.

"This morning," he continued, holding up a piece of paper, "I received a telegram from her, addressed personally to me. In it she openly accuses her husband of murder."

Mrs. DeKok snorted. Somehow it was a very lady-like sound.

"A real she-devil."

DeKok looked at the clock over the fireplace.

"It's almost midnight," he yawned. "in a few minutes the Lorelei Express from Basel will arrive at Amsterdam Central. Among the passengers will be Stella and her baby."

"Don't you have to be there?"

DeKok shook his head.

"A qualified reception committee has been arranged."

Mrs. DeKok removed the coffee cup from her almost dozing husband's hand.

"Let's go to bed," she said.

About the Author:

Albert Cornelis Baantjer (BAANTJER) first appeared on the American literary scene in September, 1992 with "DeKok and Murder on the Menu". He was a member of the Amsterdam Municipal Police force for more than 38 years and for more than 25 years he worked Homicide out of the ancient police station at 48 Warmoes Street, on the edge of Amsterdam's Red Light District. The average tenure of an officer in "the busiest police station of Europe" is about five years. Baantjer stayed until his retirement.

His appeal in the United States has been instantaneous and praise for his work has been universal. "If there could be another Maigret-like police detective, he might well be Detective-Inspector DeKok of the Amsterdam police," according to *Bruce Cassiday* of the International Association of Crime Writers. "It's easy to understand the appeal of Amsterdam police detective DeKok," writes *Charles Solomon* of the Los Angeles Times. Baantjer has been described as "a Dutch Conan Doyle" (Publishers Weekly) and has been called "a new major voice in crime fiction in America" (*Ray B. Browne*, CLUES: A Journal of Detection).

Perhaps part of the appeal is because much of Baantjer's fiction is based on real-life (or death) situations encountered during his long police career. He writes with the authority of an expert and with the compassion of a person who has seen too much suffering. He's been there.

The critics and the public have been quick to appreciate the charm and the allure of Baantjer's work. Seven "DeKok's" have been used by the (Dutch) Reader's Digest in their series of condensed books (called "Best Books" in Holland). In his native Holland, with a population of less than 15 million people, Baantjer has sold more than 5 million books and according to the Netherlands Library Information Service, a Baantjer/DeKok is checked out of a library more than 700,000 times per year.

American reviews suggest that Baantjer may become as popular in English as he is already in Dutch.

TW**I**STED

CAHROUL CRAMER

As the Chief of Homicide, the newly promoted Lieutenant Turner Fleece was expected to act as a supervisor and not as an investigator. But when an up and coming recording artist and her lover are brutally murdered in the woman's San Francisco home, the thrill of the hunt is more than Fleece can resist. He is seductively led through a maze of deceit and corruption. And at the very moment when it seems he has untangled the mystery, he realizes it has only become more twisted.

SBN 1-886411-82-9
LCCN: 97-42995
$9.95

The Cop Was White As Snow

Joyce Spizer

THE COP'S SUICIDE on a lonely beach confirmed his guilt. He had been skimming cocaine from police impounds and selling it to drug dealers to support his own habit and a growing taste for luxury. But he was Mel's Dad, and she was not about to accept this for a minute. Her Dad was no dirty cop!

THE COP WAS WHITE AS SNOW is a fast read. Spizer does a good job of keeping the action coming. Her insight as an investigator resonates throughout the book.
—Barbara Seranell, author of **No Human Involved**

JOYCE SPIZER is the shamus she writes about. The novels in the Harbour Pointe Mystery Series are fictionalized accounts of cases she has investigated. A member of Sisters in Crime, she hobnobs regularly with other mystery writers. She lives in Southern California with her husband and co-investigator, Harold.

SBN 1-886411-83-7
LCCN: 97-39430
$10.95

DEADLY DREAMS
by Gerald A. Schiller

It was happening again . . . the mist . . . struggling to find her way. Then . . . the images . . . grotesque, distorted figures under plastic sheeting, and white-coated, masked figures moving toward her . . .

When Denise Burton's recurring nightmares suddenly begin to take shape in reality, she is forced to begin a search . . . a search to discover the truth behind these horrific dreams.

The search will lead her into a series of dangerous encounters . . . in a desert ghost-town, within the restricted laboratories of Marikem, the chemical company where she works, with a brutal drug dealer and with a lover who is not what he seems.

A riveting thriller.

A thriller of fear and retaliation, *Gary Phillips,* **author of Perdition, USA;** . . . promising gambits .. a *Twilight Zone* appetizer, **Kirkus Reviews;** . . . a brisk, dialogue-driven story of nasty goings-on and cover-ups in the labs of a giant chemical works with a perky, attractive, imperiled heroine, *Charles Champlin* [Los Angeles Times].

ISBN 1-881164-81-0 / $9.95

Gerald Schiller's latest book, **DEATH UNDERGROUND,** will be available in Spring, 1999.

VOICE OF REASON . . . VOICE OF DEATH
by Gerald A. Schiller

When Cal Tech Professor Marcus Kominsky gets a frantic call from fellow teacher David Torelli, he is surprised to hear his friend exhibiting an overwhelming sense of fear. When he visits him and discovers that Torelli is being harassed by threatening notes signed by "the committee of retribution," he quickly recognizes the man may well be in imminent danger.

But Torelli is not the only one receiving the threats, and, in more than one case, the threats have culminated in murder.

Once again Kominsky, reporter Rogers Kennison, Denise Burton, and her ex-husband Donald will find themselves enmeshed in a complex web of violence, hate, fear, and death. And all of it will build to a dramatic and frightening conclusion.

This compelling thriller will be available soon from InterContinental Publishing.

Other Books from Intercontinental Publishing:

TENERIFE! by Elsinck
A fascinating study of a troubled mind. Not for the squeamish.
Contains graphic descriptions of explicit sex and violence.
ISBN 1-881164-51-9 / **$7.95**

MURDER BY FAX by Elsinck
The reader follows the alleged motives and criminal goals of the
perpetrators via a series of approximately 200 fax messages. A
technical tour-de-force building an engrossing and frightening
picture of the uses and mis-uses of modern communication
methods. ISBN 1-881164-52-7 / **$7.95**

CONFESSION OF A HIRED KILLER by Elsinck
An inside look at the Mafia and especially its devastating effect
on Italy and the rest of the world. The book is separated into three
parts: THE INVESTIGATION, THE TRANSFER and THE
CONFESSION. As actual as today's headlines!
ISBN 1-881164-53-5 / **$8.95**

VENGEANCE: Prelude to Saddam's War / Bob Mendes
A riveting "faction-thriller" by Golden Noose Winner Mendes.
Exposes Iraq's plans to become a major world power before the
Gulf War and the events leading up to Operation Desert Storm.
ISBN 1-881164-71-3 / **$9.95**

DEADLY DREAMS by Gerald Schiller
A seemingly innocuous research laboratory in the San Fernando
Valley hides a terrible secret: Experimentation on living human
beings. Denise Burton, a secretary, wonders why the graveyard
is so immaculate and why the dates on the headstones are all the
same. ISBN 1-881164-81-0 / $9.95

These and other fine books from Intercontinental Publishing are:

**Available in your Bookstore or from
Intercontinental Publishing
P.O. Box 7242
Fairfax Station, VA 22039**

Murder in Amsterdam
Baantjer

The two very first "DeKok" stories for the first time in a single volume, containing *DeKok and the Sunday Strangler* and *DeKok and the Corpse on Christmas Eve.*

First American edition of these European Best-Sellers in a single volume.
Second Printing

From critical reviews of **Murder in Amsterdam**:

If there could be another Maigret-like police detective, he might well be Detective-Inspector DeKok of the Amsterdam police. Similarities to Simenon abound in any critical judgement of Baantjer's work (*Bruce Cassiday*, **International Association of Crime Writers**); The two novellas make an irresistible case for the popularity of the Dutch author. DeKok's maverick personality certainly makes him a compassionate judge of other outsiders and an astute analyst of antisocial behavior (*Marilyn Stasio*, **The New York Times Book Review**); Both stories are very easy to take (**Kirkus Reviews**); Inspector DeKok is part Columbo, part Clouseau, part genius, and part imp. Baantjer has managed to create a figure hapless and honorable, bozoesque and brilliant, but most importantly, a body for whom the reader finds compassion (*Steven Rosen*, **West Coast Review of Books**); Readers of this book will understand why the author is so popular in Holland. His DeKok is a complex, fascinating individual (*Ray Browne*, **CLUES: A Journal of Detection**); This first translation of Baantjer's work into English supports the mystery writer's reputation in his native Holland as a Dutch Conan Doyle. His knowledge of esoterica rivals that of Holmes, but Baantjer wisely uses such trivia infrequently, his main interests clearly being detective work, characterization and moral complexity (**Publishers Weekly**).

ISBN: 1-881164-00-4
LCCN: 96-36722
$9.95

ALSO FROM INTERCONTINENTAL PUBLISHING:

The "DeKok" series by Baantjer.

If there could be another Maigret-like police detective, he might well be Detective-Inspector DeKok of the Amsterdam police. Similarities to Simenon abound in any critical judgement of Baantjer's work (*Bruce Cassiday*, **International Association of Crime Writers**); DeKok's maverick personality certainly makes him a compassionate judge of other outsiders and an astute analyst of antisocial behavior (*Marilyn Stasio*, **The New York Times Book Review**); DeKok is part Columbo, part Clouseau, part genius, and part imp. (*Steven Rosen*, **West Coast Review of Books**); It's easy to understand the appeal of Amsterdam police detective DeKok (*Charles Solomon*, **Los Angeles Times**); DeKok is a careful, compassionate policeman in the tradition of Maigret (**Library Journal**); This series is the answer to an insomniac's worst fears (*Robin W. Winks*, **The Boston Globe**).

The following Baantjer/DeKok books are currently in print:

MURDER IN AMSTERDAM (contains complete text of *DeKok and the Sunday Strangler* and *DeKok and the Corpse on Christmas Eve*);
DEKOK AND THE SOMBER NUDE
DEKOK AND THE DEAD HARLEQUIN
DEKOK AND THE SORROWING TOMCAT
DEKOK AND THE DISILLUSIONED CORPSE
DEKOK AND THE CAREFUL KILLER
DEKOK AND THE ROMANTIC MURDER
DEKOK AND THE DYING STROLLER
DEKOK AND THE CORPSE AT THE CHURCH WALL
DEKOK AND THE DANCING DEATH
DEKOK AND THE NAKED LADY
DEKOK AND THE BROTHERS OF THE EASY DEATH
DEKOK AND THE DEADLY ACCORD
DEKOK AND MURDER IN SEANCE
DEKOK AND MURDER IN ECSTASY
DEKOK AND THE BEGGING DEATH
DEKOK AND MURDER ON THE MENU.

Available soon: **DeKok and the Geese of Death** and more . . .
Available in your bookstore. U.S. distribution by IPG, Chicago, IL.